Creature
OF THE Mists

Children's Books by
Sigmund Brouwer
FROM BETHANY HOUSE PUBLISHERS

www.coolreading.com

Creature
OF THE Mists

SIGMUND BROUWER

BETHANYHOUSE

MINNEAPOLIS, MINNESOTA

Published by Bethany House Publishers
11400 Hampshire Avenue South
Bloomington, Minnesota 55438
www.bethanyhouse.com

Bethany House Publishers is a Division of
Baker Book House Company, Grand Rapids, Michigan.

Printed in the United States of America

Library of Congress Cataloging-in-Publication Data

Brouwer, Sigmund, 1959-
    Creature of the mists / by Sigmund Brouwer.
      p. cm. — (Accidental detectives)
    Summary: Searching for a fabled lake creature in Canada, Ricky and his friends come to realize that without God, faith in science is empty.
    ISBN 0-7642-2569-3 (pbk.)
    [1. Mystery and detective stories. 2. Sea monsters—Fiction. 3. Christian life—Fiction.] I. Title. II. Series: Brouwer, Sigmund, 1959-   . Accidental detectives.
    PZ7.B79984Cr   2003
    [Fic]—dc21   2003001931

SIGMUND BROUWER is the award-winning author of scores of books. He speaks to kids around the continent in an effort to instill good reading and writing habits in the next generation. Sigmund and his wife, Cindy Morgan, divide their time between Tennessee and Alberta, Canada.

For Olivia
and the sunshine you bring
into this world

CHAPTER 1

Nothing like stopping at a friend's house the morning after you have tricked him into screaming out his window loud enough to wake up the entire neighborhood.

"Morning, Ralphy. How's it going?" I said as I walked down the stairs into his basement.

Three fluorescent lights hung above him in the area his parents had made for him to repair and dismantle computers. He looked up from his cluttered worktable, eyes wide.

"Didn't you hear? I was nearly attacked by a ghost last night!"

"Get out of here!" I said with shock. "A ghost?!"

He nodded, his white, skinny face looking whiter and skinnier than usual. Hair uncombed and sticking straight up, shirt far too large and hanging out his pants, and a shy grin. That's Ralphy Zee. Computer genius and bundle of nerves.

"A scary, mean one. Right outside my window."

"It couldn't have been anything else?" I was serious now, very concerned.

"Outside a second-floor window in midair? Pale enough to see through and moaning horrible moans?"

Those moans had been Mike Andrews' idea. For someone who hates work and school, Mike has a lot of energy to misplace.

"A ghost!" I repeated. "What did it look like? What time? What did you do?"

Ralphy shook his head and sighed to remember his terror. And what terror it had been. By the time he had finished screaming, lights had flicked on in every house on the block.

"It was big and pale with eyes like fire. Just before midnight." He stopped and lowered his voice to a whisper. "Don't you see? Midnight, on a Friday. On a Friday the Thirteenth. All I could do was scream for help."

Served him right for letting superstition get to him. Even if Mike and I had spent the entire Friday evening beforehand telling him ghost stories.

"Did it say anything?" My eyes grew as wide as his.

He gulped. "It said it was a ghost of a soldier from the Civil War. That it only appeared on Friday the Thirteenth. That I should stay awake waiting for it on the next Friday the Thirteenth."

I whistled. "No kidding. Maybe Mike and I should be with you then for support. Did it say anything else?"

"Something about leaving my video game collection some-where." His face grew even more troubled. "I hope it doesn't hurt me. I didn't catch the exact directions."

Nuts. I told Mike he was talking too quickly.

I shook my head. "Told your parents yet?"

"Yes," he said mournfully. "They won't let me read scary books anymore."

I shook my head again, but not at Ralphy's parents. At Ralphy. Ever notice that people who get scared easily are the ones who just have to watch horror shows and read gruesome books?

"That's too bad," I said. "Wait till Mike hears about this."

Ralphy sighed again and resumed his careful work with com-puter parts. I watched in silence. Not that I understood anything he was doing.

On one end he had the old screen from a portable television. In the middle, set clearly apart from the clutter of tools and small parts, there was a wide wooden tray with small black chips and soldered wire in all directions. On the far end sat what looked like a car battery sliced in half.

"Inventing something?" I asked half jokingly.

Ralphy grunted at a wire he was trying to clip. "Yup. I'd like to win the statewide science contest."

"What's first prize? A set of encyclopedias?" I nearly choked with glee.

"Good one, Ricky Kidd." He continued to work.

When they use your last name, it's a safe bet the remark was sarcastic. Finally I said, "Well?"

"Well what?" He didn't look up.

"What's first prize?"

"A trip this summer. To the Okanogan Valley of British Columbia."

"British Columbia. That's a province in Canada."

"Uh-huh," he said absently. "It's kind of a publicity thing. Some oceanographer has invented a new deep-sea scanner. He'll be searching for the Ogopogo monster, a cousin to the Loch Ness monster in Scotland. The company sponsoring this oceanographer wants some school kids along to give the expedition a better image."

I snorted. "An Ogopogo monster in the Okanogan. Hah, hah. You should learn to tell better lies." *And back them up with great inventions,* I thought, *like the ghost Mike and I spent so long making.*

Ralphy shrugged as he dabbed something in front of him. "Do me a favor, Ricky. Hold these two wires."

"No problem."

I took one in each hand. They felt damp, but it only lasted for a few seconds.

"Thanks," he said mildly as he moved to the far end of the table and reached for a small handle attached to a cylinder the size of a football.

He began to crank.

"Yeeeeeooooooooowwwww!" I hollered and tried to shake the wires loose.

Ralphy stopped cranking.

"Oh," he said. "Glad to see it works."

He cranked again.

It felt like sharks were biting my hands. Each crank of Ralphy's hand produced another vicious nip. "That's electricity!" I shouted above the numbing pain.

Ralphy stopped cranking. "Good. I was worried I hadn't set the circuits up properly."

The wires still wouldn't shake loose. Not that my fingers could move at this point anyway.

He cranked again. "Ralphy!" I shouted. "Have you lost your mind?!"

He stopped and thought about it. "Nope." He cranked again.

"Yeeeeeoooooowwwww!"

"It's only a couple of volts," he noted at the next stop. "Nothing that will really hurt you. But the superglue I used will make the wires hard to shake loose."

I plucked at the wires. Ralphy *had* gone crazy.

He cranked again until I stopped plucking.

Ralphy grinned at me. "Now, about last night," he said.

My jaw dropped.

"You know?"

He kept grinning and raised his voice. "Lisa, you can come out now. And bring your friends."

Wonderful. Lisa Higgins was in on this? She's the kind of girl you dread. Pretty, with long dark hair. When she smiles, it's sunshine breaking through clouds. When she scowls, it's a thunderstorm. She's the girl who hits home runs off your best pitches, beats you in math tests, and always catches you in the middle of something stupid.

Like right now.

She stepped out of the basement closet and flashed her teeth in a grin at me. Then she turned around and hauled out one of her friends—a large figure made from helium-filled balloons.

I closed my eyes in grief.

Nobody had to tell me what that was. Less than twelve hours earlier, Mike and I had stood outside Ralphy's window and floated it up on invisible nylon fishing line. A miniature speaker was attached to the base of the balloons, and where the eyes were, we had taped two tiny pen-sized flashlights.

I smiled weakly. "You would have been proud of us, Ralphy. It took three weeks for us to put it together. Cost nearly twenty bucks for all the parts."

I stopped. "Hey!" I said with indignation. "How did you find out, anyway?"

Lisa's other friend, the answer to my question, stepped out of the closet.

Joel and his teddy bear. How he manages to follow people is beyond me. He's my six-year-old kid brother, who haunts me worse than any ghost. I'm twelve, but he terrifies me. Somehow he appears and disappears when I least expect or want it. Locked doors and walls don't stop that kid. When I do spot him, he says nothing. Only stares at me with solemn eyes that take in exactly whatever I'm doing at that moment, which usually happens to be something I want nobody in the world to see. Then, as I'm bursting out of my skin in terror at his sudden appearance, he's gone again.

"Funny trick you did last night," Joel said gravely. "You and Mike gonna do it again for Lisa?"

I gritted my teeth.

"We were going to return your video games," I said hopefully, suddenly aware again of those wires stuck to my skin.

Ralphy grinned. "Actually, it was a great trick. I'll help you remove those wires, and we'll call us even."

Whew.

As he pulled them from my hands, nearly ripping skin from my palms, he explained. "The crank is part of a generator. I need to store electricity in that battery so that it will operate my homemade computer. Nearly everything is made from scratch," he finished proudly.

"You already have a new iBook laptop," I pointed out.

"For the science contest."

"Ah yes," I said in disbelief. "To go looking for an Oglipolgi."

"Ogopogo," he corrected me.

Before I could say anything, a voice from upstairs interrupted.

"Helloooo. Anybody home?" It was Mike.

Lisa and Joel backed into the closet, taking the balloons with them. I stepped into the nearby laundry room, out of sight.

Mike sauntered down the stairs. "Morning, Ralphy. How's it going?" he said.

"Didn't you hear?" Ralphy's voice trembled. "I was nearly attacked by a ghost last night!"

"No way!" Mike said with shock. "A ghost?!"

"A ghost," Ralphy repeated firmly. He paused. "Say, Mike. Could you do me a favor and hold these wires for me?"

CHAPTER 2

It was a beautiful Saturday morning three or four weeks after The Big Scare, which had become known all around our small town of Jamesville as The Big Backfire.

Around me, the trees hung heavy and green along the sidewalks. In the clean morning air, the chortling of the birds carried clearly as they staked their ownership claims by the stately old houses on both sides of the street. Summer vacation was half over, and I was feeling the urge to do some fishing. Without a certain kid brother spying on my every move.

Mike and I had easily forgiven Ralphy for outsmarting us. The superglue had taken only a few days to come off our hands, the feeling in our fingers had returned within a day, and Lisa had given us back our balloon ghost without popping it. Still, as tricks went, Mike and I had lost that round, and it was definitely Joel's fault.

Worse, I had spent every day after that jumping at the slightest sound behind my back. Joel has a habit of making a person do that. I had no idea how he had managed to follow Mike and me so quietly to Ralphy's window, but it served as a reminder that at no moment could I judge myself safe from my kid brother's conscience.

To make me more jumpy, there was the fact that Jamesville is too small to be able to escape Joel completely. The best I could do was throw his teddy bear in the dryer occasionally.

That sounds crazy, but it works. The kid can tame wild animals and move as quietly as smoke, but he has a weakness for a dumb, battered teddy bear, brown with gray-white paws, with a black button and a white button for eyes that, after popping off, always get sewn on in a mixed-up order. The teddy bear is his security blanket, and when I need to buy time, I throw it in the dryer and he patiently watches until the cycle ends.

A guy can't possibly plan for a six-year-old brother to drift out of bed on the night of Friday the Thirteenth, I told myself as I reviewed our mistake from that night. *It's unfair that*—

"Eeeeeeeek!"

I landed and turned around. "Joel, I've told you a billion times not to—oh, hi, Mike. Thanks for the heart attack."

"I only tapped you on the shoulder." He grinned. As usual, I needed sunglasses to look at him. Hawaiian shirt, mismatched sneakers, New York Yankees ball cap, and bright red hair. The kind of guy who will try to juggle chain saws as soon as you tell him it's not possible. The kind of guy whose grin earns cookies from the grumpiest of old ladies.

"You haven't seen Joel, have you?"

He snorted. "Who *ever* sees him?"

Exactly.

"Wanna head down to the river and—"

"—do some fishing," he finished.

I nodded. "Maybe we can tear Ralphy away from his books."

Mike rolled his eyeballs. "If he learns much more about that dumb lake in Canada, he'll be able to find that monster all by himself."

"He'll have to. The odds of winning that contest are so low you can bet nobody else will be taking him. I mean, half the summer is gone. You'd think he would have given up by now."

Mike snorted again. "Some guys are born optimists. Even if he does win statewide, they still have to draw his name from the winners of all the other states. You'd have to worry more about getting hit by lightning."

I nodded as we reached the downtown area of Jamesville. Downtown isn't much more than a couple of square blocks of stores and some restaurants and parking lots. We would be reaching Ralphy's house on the other side in a few minutes.

We walked past City Hall and its park with the muddy little pond in the center of a wide expanse of lawn. And once we reached the stretch of houses on the other side, we began evasive tactics to escape Joel. After all, it was a Saturday morning, and he loves nothing better than spying on us to make his day exciting.

First, a shortcut through Mrs. Thompson's garden that became a longcut—we circled the house once and came out through the hedge on the same side we entered. Sometimes that fools Joel.

Then we dashed across the school playground, hid at the corner of the school, and waited and watched for five minutes to see if we had lost Joel. Not even he can cover that much open ground without being spotted.

Finally, to be totally safe, we snuck down the alley behind Ralphy's house and crept through the bushes of his next-door neighbor to survey the situation. There we could see both the front and back of Ralphy's yard, knowing that sometimes Joel simply guesses where we're going and beats us there.

We stayed on our stomachs beneath a bush for another few minutes, craning our heads. Mike stared at the front. I kept an eagle eye on the side and what I could see of the back. This time it looked like we were in the clear—

"Pssssssssst!"

"What?" I hissed. "And do you have to spit all over my ear and neck when you do that?"

"Do what?"

"Pssssssssssst!" I turned my head in his direction and sprayed the side of his face.

"This is serious," he said without turning his head or wiping his neck. "Inch my way and tell me what you see."

I crawled a half foot closer to get his viewpoint of the front of Ralphy's house. "A motor home."

"It just pulled up," Mike said.

"Probably someone along the street is expecting visitors. It is summer, after all."

"No way." Mike said it so flatly, my skin crawled. There was a small pause as the driver's door of the motor home slammed shut. Two more seconds, then Mike's voice grew even flatter and colder. "Trouble."

I pushed a leafy branch out of my face and nearly gasped.

"He's got a huge rifle!"

"Yup. I thought I saw him reaching for it as he pulled up. That's what made me nervous. It looks like a bazooka."

My mind reeled. This was Jamesville. Things like this only happened in stories on the eleven o'clock news.

The man was dressed in shabby brown clothes. Shadows from the morning sun filled his narrow face. He wore wire-rim glasses and had a creepy way of shuffling.

"We've got to warn Ralphy!"

"How?" Mike asked. "Look. The man's three steps away from the front door."

My palms began to sweat. On Saturday mornings Ralphy is always home alone. His mom and dad work, and his two high-school-aged sisters are always off somewhere.

The chiming of the front doorbell reached us plainly.

Joel darted into view at the far edge of the front lawn, then disappeared behind an elm tree. He peeked around.

Stay away, Joel! I wanted to scream. My throat felt locked with fear.

Ralphy opened the front door, his shirt, as usual, draped nearly to his knees. His eyes bugged out at the sight of the bazooka.

"This is it," the man announced. The words rasped.

Ralphy stared at him, then stared at the rifle. There were

seconds and seconds of silence that seemed like hours each.

"I can't believe it." Ralphy's words trembled with emotion as he finally managed to speak.

Joel's head popped behind the tree, then reappeared on the other side. *Will he understand what is happening?*

"Believe it, kid. Come on, I'm taking you to the motor home."

"Motor home. Surely this is a joke? I mean, all of this—"

"You might as well get used to it, kid, because you'll be stuck in there for quite some time."

Ralphy simply nodded, stunned by the suddenness of it. I felt the same way.

They walked away from the house. The man kept the bazooka casually draped in the crook of his right arm.

Joel stepped away from the tree and waved a friendly greeting!

The man mumbled something to Ralphy, but they were too far away for me to understand. I did understand extreme danger, and that was only too obvious as the man took Joel by the hand and led him around the front of the motor home.

The door clicked shut.

It was not time to think. Whoever he was, and whatever he was doing, I couldn't allow it to become another crazy report on the late news.

"It's a kidnapping!" I said tersely.

I stood so quickly that I scraped a couple of square feet of skin against the branches above me. As the motor home's engine fired up, I began running.

I still had no idea of what I was doing. Facing the man's weapon was obvious suicide, but there was no way I wanted that vehicle out of my sight. As long as he was driving, Ralphy and Joel were safe. When he stopped—I didn't want to think about that, either. I did know, even as I was pounding along the ground, that if I waited and called the police, even a ten-minute delay might prove to be horrible.

The bumper. *Get on the bumper!*

The motor home began to pull away.

There was a pounding of feet beside me. *Good old Mike!*

Just before the motor home pulled totally out of reach, we managed to hook on to the ladder at the back and swing up and onto the bumper.

I wheezed for breath. "What next, pal?"

"We'll figure out something when it stops." He stopped to draw another gasping lungful of air. "If we last that long."

Beneath us, the pavement became a blur.

CHAPTER  3

Is this really happening?

Sure, you can imagine things when you daydream. Like how you would single-handedly stop a bank robber or rescue someone's baby from a burning house. But in daydreams, there's always a nice, fuzzy glow to your thoughts. Not wind whipping your hair against your face while your heart skips every second beat in fear.

"What if he gets to a highway?" Mike shouted above the growing roar from the motor home's exhaust pipe.

Suddenly I saw our solution clearly.

"Perfect!" I shouted back. "We'll get pulled over by the police!"

I grinned. It wouldn't take long for us to leave these quiet streets and for a motorist to spot us. Then it was only a matter of time until a state patrol officer stopped the motor home and rescued Ralphy and Joel. We'd finally find out what possessed this lunatic to kidnap them out of the blue.

Except the motor home began to slow down.

Mike and I frowned at each other. We had barely reached City Hall Park.

The motor home rumbled to a stop. The driver's door clicked open.

I held my breath. *What if he walks around the back?*

"I'm sorry, kid," came the rasping voice. "It's got to be the pond."

"What about Joel?" Ralphy asked bravely. It put a lump in my throat. Some maniac was going to do something crazy to him with a bazooka, and Ralphy's concern was the safety of my brother.

"He's too young to understand. As far as I'm concerned, he can do what he wants."

"I'll send him home, then," Ralphy said. The lump in my throat grew bigger.

Seconds later, Joel wandered around the corner of the motor home. I grabbed him from behind as he walked past, and cupped my hand over his mouth.

Joel did not struggle. He did not drop his teddy bear.

He bit.

I kept the scream in my throat down to a muffled grunt.

"It's me," I whispered. "Don't worry."

He calmly bit again. Some gratitude.

I hissed into his ear, "Joel, run home and tell Mom to get help and meet us here! Got it?"

I let go before he could bite again, then held my breath and waited.

Joel is as unpredictable as a fox. He looked at me once, kicked dirt on my shoes, then turned around and walked away with dignity, even as his teddy bear trailed from his left hand.

I had more immediate things to worry about.

We were on the street alongside the park. There were maybe a hundred yards to the pond. Ralphy and the maniac would be halfway there by now. I could think of nothing good that might happen with a bazooka-toting lunatic holding a friend of mine as hostage.

Sometimes fear makes you think clearly. A solution so simple hit me that I almost forgot to breathe.

"Mike! Follow me!"

I crept around the side of the motor home without waiting.

Please be there, I pleaded silently as I cracked open the door of the motor home. *Be there in the ignition.*

It was. The key.

I motioned for Mike to get inside.

I followed and pushed him onto the passenger side.

"Are you nuts?" he asked as I climbed behind the steering wheel.

"Can you think of anything better?"

Silence.

I took a deep breath, then turned the key.

Twelve-year-olds do not get driver's licenses. But all of us have seen enough to know you throw the car into gear. The brake pedal is on the left. Gas pedal on the right. All you do is steer. And I was going to steer right into them. It would give Ralphy a chance to run away.

"Here we go, pal," I said, trying to be cool. It didn't work. My voice broke on the word *pal.*

I pulled the lever toward me and slid it into D, for Drive.

The motor home lurched forward.

We were committed to action. We were also about to rescue our friend.

It hit me like a fierce joy, the adrenaline of being so bold. I gave my best kamikaze yell and hit the gas pedal.

Whooooommmmmppp. The motor home surged forward.

I cranked the wheel just in time to miss a tree, and we were on the park grass and picking up speed.

Hoooonnnnkkkkk! Hoooooooonnnnkkkkk!

The maniac turned, his white face plastered with amazement. Ralphy's jaw dropped.

Perched high above and looking down from the window, we roared forward, quickly closing the gap. With too much speed.

"The brakes, Ricky! The brakes!" Mike shouted.

I slammed down hard, and the motor home slewed a quarter turn sideways on the slick grass as we flashed past them.

The steering wheel nearly flung me into the door.

I straightened in time to crank us directly through the middle of a bunch of rose bushes. We clipped forward and found more open grass.

Had it worked? Had we managed to split the two of them?

The motor home made a slow turn that took twenty agonizing seconds as I fed it more gas.

Yes! The bazooka was on the ground, and both of them were fleeing in opposite directions.

"I'll get him now!" I shouted as the motor home picked up speed. Deep tracks in the grass showed clearly our first run. "See if he kidnaps any more kids!"

"Ricky," Mike shouted back. "Stop!"

"Hah, hah!" I screamed as the adrenaline filled me completely. "First I run over his bazooka! Then him!"

"Ricky!" Mike jumped across and pulled the steering wheel hard to the right so that we narrowly missed the terrible weapon on the ground in front of us.

Had he lost his mind?

We fought for the wheel and crashed through another set of rose bushes. The pond decided our outcome. It got in our way.

The front half of the motor home dropped suddenly as it slid on the mud along the bank.

The silence was terrible as the engine stalled and the huge vehicle settled wheel-high in water.

Springs creaked briefly, then that, too, quit.

Finally Mike croaked out some words. "Life as we know it has just ended."

I blinked. "You're right. We're heroes." One less weirdo would be making the news for doing something terrible to a kid. We would be the ones in the paper instead. "Everyone will forgive us for this mess. Medals, newspaper articles—"

"Exactly," Mike said. "Newspaper articles."

He handed me a paper from a pile beside the console. I tried to comprehend the blaring headlines across the Saturday morning edition of the *Jamesville Herald.*

WORLD-RENOWNED SCIENTIST VISITS TOWN

Local boy wins expedition contest

There, staring back at me, was a picture of the man I had just tried to mow down with his own motor home.

CHAPTER 4

"Look," Ralphy said, his eyes briefly flashing anger. "You guys laughed every time I mentioned the science contest. You never gave me a chance to tell you more about it. Or about Dr. Wineguard."

He had just walked over from the pond. Mike and I were standing by the crushed rose bushes, well away from the accident scene, as if somehow that made us less responsible.

Over Ralphy's shoulder, I watched a tow truck back up slowly to the rear end of the motor home. A small crowd had already gathered around it. I dreaded the moment a grown-up would detach himself from that group and head our way.

"Ralphy," I moaned. "This is serious trouble." I pictured Mike and me standing in front of a judge. *"Driving without a license. Reckless driving. Attempt to injure.* The charges will go on and on. Not to mention how much this will cost in damages. You should have let us know *something* about this guy."

Ralphy shook his head as if to clear it of cobwebs. "I didn't know until this morning when he called. From a phone booth in Jamesville. When I tried calling to let you guys know, your mothers said you were gone."

"We were on our way to your house," Mike said in

defense.

"How were we to know that he wasn't a kidnapper?" I added.

"How was I supposed to know you guys were spying?"

"But the bazooka," I protested. "A guy walks up to your house and points a bazooka at you."

"It's a Sonar Scanner. I already explained a dozen times. His latest invention. He uses it to focus sonar waves, much like the depth finders fishermen use. Except this one is so accurate, it's like using a telescope to look deep into the water."

"I know, I know," I groaned. "And on the phone, you told him the only water nearby for him to demonstrate it was at this park, and—"

Ralphy nodded impatiently. "And thanks to you guys, I still haven't seen it in action. The principle behind it is so simple, it's incredible no one thought of it years ago. Dr. Wineguard was telling me that—"

Ralphy was getting that scientific fervor in his eyes.

"Stop!" I said. "Any second Mike and I will be arrested and thrown in jail forever. I don't *want* to hear about inventions or experiments or traveling scientists."

I stopped, groaned louder, and covered my face with my hands. It didn't help. When I opened my eyes, my mom was still there. As the tow truck slowly winched up the back end of the motor home, she moved in the direction of Dr. Wineguard, who was still standing and staring at the front end of his vehicle.

They began talking. I felt like throwing up.

Two eternities later, Mom went over to discuss things with the tow truck driver, who was nearly ready to begin hauling the motor home out of the pond. Dr. Wineguard ambled in our direction.

I winced. "Here it comes, Mike," I said under my breath. "Like you said, the end of life as we know it."

Dr. Wineguard stopped directly in front of us and stared at us fully before speaking. Close up, he still looked shabby. He ran his fingers back through his scraggly, thin hair to keep it from falling in his eyes, which had dark rings under them. His nose was long and almost pointed, and his glasses seemed perched there. If his entire body was as skinny as his neck, I could understand why the shapeless brown clothing he wore fit him like loose clothes on a wire hanger.

"Which one of you is Richard Kidd?" he asked in the raspy voice that had made me quake with adrenaline and fear when he had first addressed Ralphy on the doorstep.

I raised my hand, trying not to show terror.

"You're the one with the hyper imagination," he commented blandly, as if discussing an insect under a microscope. "The one who wants to be a writer."

Mothers always embarrass a person.

"Yes, sir."

"Let me guess," he said. "You thought I was kidnapping your friend."

I gulped. "And my brother." I went on in a rush of words. "You hear about so many weirdos in the news, sir. Losing their minds. Firing guns in restaurants. Taking hostages. Crazy people doing crazy things. I saw that baz—I mean Sonar Scanner—and thought—"

"Thought I was a crazy," he finished quietly.

My ears began to burn as the blood hit my face. "Yes. I mean, no. I mean, it really does look like a bazooka."

"So you decided to steal my own vehicle and run me down."

I looked at the ground. *Why do these things always happen to me?* Less than an hour ago, my biggest problem was losing Joel and finding a way to fish in peace.

"I said," he repeated, "you decided to steal my own vehicle and run me down."

I looked up and felt my jaw tighten with anger as I remembered how scared I had been for Ralphy and Joel. "Yes, sir." More anger hit me. "Yes, sir, I did." I couldn't stop my thoughts from tumbling out. "Now that I think about it, it wasn't such a dumb gamble. If you weren't a crazy, the worst that happens is whatever you choose to do to me now. But if you *were* a crazy, and I did nothing, the worst that could have happened might have been something much more terrible to my friend and to my brother. Looking at it that way, it was a risk worth taking. Even though I lost."

I ran out of breath and, suddenly realizing how forceful I had been, turned red from chin to forehead again.

"Well spoken," he said quietly. "A certain logic there is quite admirable. Better safe than sorry, I believe is what you mean."

I nodded, still expecting to get yelled at.

"Well," he said, running his hand through his hair again. "I'm glad that's all cleared up."

His gaze drifted into the distance and he sighed. "Stress like this sure makes me miss a cigarette, though."

He refocused on Mike and Ralphy and me. "We might as well get right down to business. After all, that's why I'm here in person. We have less than a week to get to the lake."

Mike coughed gently. "Excuse me, sir. You mean you won't throw us in jail?"

"Huh? Jail. Oh, jail. Of course not. That's nonsense. No one was hurt, and you had a perfectly reasonable explanation for what you did. After all, that's what science is about. Reasonable explanations."

He grinned as our jaws dropped. It was the first time I had seen him smile, and the change on his angular face was remarkable. "Come now," he said through his suddenly warm grin. "Insurance will cover the damages. And if I don't press charges, that's the end of that."

"You, you won't try to punish—" My voice broke with surprise, so I didn't try any more words. I hated it when it did that to me.

He waved a long finger at us. "Besides, if I put you two in jail, it would create bad feelings. And expedition members can't have bad feelings for each other."

I rubbed my ears, trying to clear them. *Did he say...*

Mike asked my question for me. "Expedition members?"

"Of course," he said with impatience. "Certainly you knew about all of this when you helped Ralphy with his science project. You all won together. You all go to the Okanogan together. It's that simple."

I sat on the grass before my body decided to faint.

CHAPTER 5

"Let me get this straight," I said to Ralphy. "Mike, Lisa, and I helped you rig up a homemade computer."

We were alone in the park. The tow truck had taken the motor home and Dr. Wineguard to Scope's Automotive Repair. The crowd of spectators had dispersed. Mom had left, Joel firmly in hand, saying only that we would have a discussion later. The sun was shining high in a blue sky, and the only signs of my previous panic were some shredded rose bushes, tire tracks mashed into the grass, and the skid marks leading down to the pond. I had a feeling I'd be twenty-one before anybody would let me behind a steering wheel again.

I decided to worry about that later. Our entire gang had the chance to track down a lake monster before the end of the week.

I continued my question before Ralphy could reply. "And you put our names on the contest entry without telling us?"

"You guys aren't mad, are you?"

"Mad?" I looked at Mike. "Are we mad?"

Mike kept a serious face. "Hopping mad, Ralphy. I had planned to spend the next week of my summer vacation doing something exciting. Like watching grass grow."

Ralphy frowned with thought. "That could work.

Measure off four test plots. Water the first. Fertilize the second. Water and fertilize the third. Then compare the rate of each one's growth to the fourth patch, which you leave alone. Then graph the growth rate and extrapolate it in segments of—"

"Ralphy," I interrupted the scientific glow that was heating up his face. "I think Mike was being sarcastic. We're both dying to look for an Oglipogli. We just want to know exactly what we did to be part of your science team."

Relief broke his frown into a grin. "Ogopogo. Not Oglipogli. It's a huge sea serpent, some think related to the Loch Ness monster, that has been sighted many times, first by the local Indians, then by a white man in the Okanogan Valley in—"

"Ralphy! How did we help you build the computer that won the contest?"

He grinned apologetically. "You held the wires and tested my generator for electricity. Remember? The morning after that ghost attack, when I glued the wires with—"

"Yeah, yeah," Mike said quickly. Neither of us liked thinking about it. "That was enough to put us on the team?"

"Enough in my book. I sure wouldn't want to go on something like this without you guys. After all, what are friends for?"

What a way to make a person feel bad. We had laughed and teased him about the contest for weeks, and all along he had planned to let us share in it.

"We owe you, Ralphy."

"Shucks, it was nothing."

"Really," Mike said. "After the rough time we gave you about the contest, too. If there was ever anything we could do to pay you back . . ."

Ralphy looked at the ground and shuffled his feet. "Pay me back for a ten-day expedition? I wouldn't think of it. Not even if it is all expenses paid with a world-famous oceanographer."

I should have smelled the steel of a trap right then.

"Are you kidding?" I said. "We owe you a dozen favors. Right, Mike?"

"Right," he said, satisfied that now we had thanked Ralphy enough.

We turned to leave the park and get on with the rest of the Saturday.

"A dozen favors, huh," Ralphy contemplated.

"Two dozen," Mike said firmly.

"Well," Ralphy began. "I was supposed to paint the fence today, and I was hoping I could spend some more time studying before we left . . ."

"Paint the fence?" Mike gulped.

"Only three coats. But if you guys think that's too much to ask . . ."

The trap snapped shut.

Our trip to Canada ended up costing Mike and me a dozen blisters, two sunburned backs, and all the Popsicles required to keep Joel away from the paint cans.

CHAPTER 6

Tuesday already. Things had happened so quickly, I could still hardly believe I was about to travel across the country in the same motor home that I had so recently driven into the City Hall pond.

Our entire crew was gathered in front of Ralphy's house. Mike Andrews, with his Yankees ball cap twisted slightly to the side. Ralphy, looking excited and scared at the same time. Lisa Higgins, with faded blue jeans and a T-shirt, just like the rest of us.

And me, trying to duck a good-bye kiss.

"Mom," I hissed. "Why do you have to do this in front of everyone?"

"Because I know it drives you nuts." She smiled sweetly. "Besides, I'm not sure I've forgiven you for that stunt in the park last Saturday."

"I was trying to save Joel," I protested for the hundredth time.

She leaned forward and kissed me again as she corrected me. "Your hyperactive imagination was trying to save Joel."

I ducked enough to get her kiss on my forehead.

"Some gratitude he's got," I grumbled. "Not even being here to see us off."

"You know your brother. Here one minute. Gone the

next. He walked with me halfway, then disappeared. It's a good thing he knows when lunch is served."

"Say good-bye to him for me," I said as a wave of affection for the little squirt hit me. "Who knows, I might even end up missing him." I knew I would also miss my little sister, Rachel. She was taking a nap right now, but I'd already kissed her forehead and whispered a good-bye to her.

"Right," Mom replied with grave disbelief. "Now go. Dr. Wineguard is waving all of you aboard."

She paused, then placed her hands on my shoulders, a sure sign of seriousness. "Ricky, you can trust Dr. Wineguard. He may seem eccentric, but he's a good man, and he's a Christian. There is no way we would be letting you go otherwise."

I snorted, even as the others started toward the motor home. "Mom, he only came for Sunday dinner at our place. How can you know that for sure?"

Not that I wanted her to be wrong. Without my parents' permission, I wouldn't be going. But you have to keep them on their toes once in a while.

She smiled the same mysterious smile Lisa Higgins uses to drive me nuts. "Because I also called his university chaplain yesterday for a complete background check. After all, you will be traveling nearly two thousand miles with the man to get there. Somebody has to look out for you."

"Oh."

She gave me a slap on the rear end to hurry me on. *Mothers.*

Our gear was already stowed in a rear compartment on the outside of the motor home. When I joined the others inside and Dr. Wineguard pulled aside a curtain to the back part of the vehicle, I saw why our gear needed to be outside. Something I had been too full of adrenaline to notice when I had slid behind the steering wheel the Saturday before.

What I saw now were computers. Computer screens. Computer

tables. More computers. Half the motor home was devoted to a mini-laboratory.

"Not much," Dr. Wineguard said dryly at our obvious astonishment, "but I call it home."

Ralphy almost swooned. No other word will work. He swooned as if he were a knight meeting his true love.

"This is paradise," he breathed.

"A lot of it is necessary to operate the programs for my Sonar Scanner," Dr. Wineguard explained. "You would have seen it Saturday, except more than just the scanner managed to get a close-up of the pond. I'm glad only the front wheels went under."

My ears burned. "Sorry, Ralphy."

He didn't hear me as he darted to the first computer. "Not the latest Mac?! What's the processor speed? Or have you tinkered with the factory settings?"

"Slow down, slow down," Dr. Wineguard protested. "You've got all trip to become acquainted with the hardware. Why don't I fill all of you in on some of the rest of the details as we drive."

We did not disagree.

The left half of the motor home consisted of comfortable lounge seats. There was a television, small kitchenette, and only... only one small bed?

Dr. Wineguard hollered over his shoulder as he put the motor home into gear. "You might be wondering. This seats eight. Sleeps one. We'll be staying at motels."

Something about that nagged at me—besides the fact that he had almost read my mind—but I put it away. This was a scientific expedition. A lucky one-in-a-thousand chance for a few kids from Jamesville. Who was I to become suspicious in the first half mile?

Dr. Wineguard continued. "First of all, I'd like to review the purpose of our expedition. And no, I wasn't crazy to be picking you guys up personally. Jamesville happens to lie near the route I would be taking from my own hometown university to the lake in Canada. I was coming this way anyhow. I've got to take everything in this

motor home, because it will serve as base camp when we get there."
I noticed his small smile to himself in the rearview mirror. "Ralphy
may have told you some about the rest of our trip by now, but I
want to be on the safe side. Questions may come up later."

What did he mean by that? I did not get a chance to ask.

"We are going to be searching for a creature called the Ogopogo.
It is said to be a huge sea serpent which lives in Lake Okanogan. It
has been sighted numerous times but has never been clearly photo-
graphed or captured. There has been no solid scientific proof of its
existence. The purpose of our trip is to find that proof, thanks to
something called the Sonar Scanner."

Ralphy leaned forward.

"The scanner itself," Dr. Wineguard said as we left the outskirts
of Jamesville, "is not totally new. Sonar radar that works underwater
has been around since the Second World War. My only modification
to that was in focusing it to be sharper at much greater depths from
the surface by using a—" he chuckled—"bazooka-shaped amplifier."

Will I ever hear the end of it?

"However, what is revolutionary at this point is the computer
programming that reads the sonar input. I will immodestly tell you
that I developed a program that essentially converts the sonar blips
into signals that read like those entering a television. In other
words, it's like sending down a television camera."

Lisa scratched her head. "But, Dr. Wineguard, they already send
television cameras underwater."

"Are you guys going to question everything?"

Embarrassed silence from all of us.

Dr. Wineguard turned his head briefly, enough to flash a grin
from his angular face before watching the highway again. "I hope
so," he said. "That's science. Questions looking for reasonable explanations."

The motor home rumbled forward. Already we had left the
familiar river valley that held Jamesville and were almost to the
interstate that headed west.

It was a gray day, skies threatening rain but holding off, and little wind. Perfect traveling weather, Dr. Wineguard had said, not too hot, not too cold, and only ten hours of driving before our first stop in Minneapolis.

"Hang on a second before I answer that, Lisa." Dr. Wineguard concentrated on taking the motor home smoothly from the on-ramp into the traffic flowing along the interstate highway.

"Okay," he said. "About television cameras. They are only as good as the light around them. No light, no vision. No vision, no television camera. The scanner, on the other hand, works to almost any depth. Plus, it works from the surface. Saves cumbersome and expensive diving."

I looked around the interior of the motor home, wondering again what it was nagging at me. Nothing jumped out. Ralphy was still leaning forward in his seat. Mike, cap now straight, lolled back against his cushions. Lisa watched the passing countryside with thoughtful eyes as she listened to Dr. Wineguard.

The computer equipment was anchored solidly to the opposite wall, and our big vehicle hummed smoothly.

Equipment!

It struck me. *Money!* We were riding in a motor home worth maybe a quarter of a million dollars, with equipment that probably cost an equal amount. Expedition expenses—motels, restaurants, gasoline—would be no small peanuts.

My dad always told me that nobody does anything for nothing, not in the real world of business. Who was paying for all of this? And why?

My suspicions grew stronger. It was nice to be the winners of this contest, but why spend all this money on kids?

So I tried fishing around for the answer. "Um, Dr. Wineguard, this is the first real test of the Sonar Scanner?"

"Yes, sir," he replied cheerfully.

"All of this must have cost a bundle. The research and every-thing?"

He nodded without turning.

"Wouldn't it pay, then, to use it on something practical?" I thought of the pirate stories I'd been reading recently. "Like recovering lost treasures?"

"Ho, ho!" he cried. "You guys are sharper than you look. That's a very good question."

I hoped he would give a very good answer.

"To find lost treasure," he stated, "you are looking for a needle in a haystack. The ocean is huge, and the bottom is often incredibly far below. Looking for treasure would be like searching hundreds of square miles of land from an airplane, seeking something very tiny from a great distance above the ground. To make it worse, that small target is probably covered with growing grass or drifting sand. The only way to stumble across it is with a map, and if you have a map, you certainly don't need the Sonar Scanner.

"Furthermore, once you do find it, there is considerable trouble in recovering it. Diving crews can only go so deep. And all of that costs extra money."

I remained silent. So far, he hadn't given me much to silence my doubts. *Why the Ogopogo monster? Why with kids?*

So I asked the first question out loud. I wasn't sure I was ready for an answer to the second.

Dr. Wineguard strummed the steering wheel. "Why the Ogopogo?" he repeated. "Why spend all this money on what may be merely a legend?"

I nodded again.

"Two reasons," he said. "I am, after all, an oceanographer. I pursue the scientific knowledge of marine creatures. I really do want to prove it exists and show that it is related to a species of reptiles thought long extinct."

I was willing to bet the second reason involved money.

"However, research doesn't come cheap. Not even with a university backing you. Compudel, a large private computer development company, has sunk hundreds of thousands of dollars into this, and they want the dividends."

Mike blurted, "I can't see an Ogopogo earning you money. Fame, maybe, but not fortune."

"I see." Dr. Wineguard rubbed his chin thoughtfully. "How's this for an answer. There's a town on Lake Okanogan with a tourism gimmick that consists of a prize to anyone who might be able to prove the Ogopogo exists."

"Your photograph in the local newspaper," Mike suggested. "That's the prize."

Ralphy frowned. He didn't want anyone making fun of any of this.

"Nope," Dr. Wineguard replied, noticing Ralphy's frown in the rearview mirror. "Enough money to make even a dedicated scientist take notice."

He paused, then said, "One million dollars."

I don't think I can be blamed for forgetting about my second question until we stepped out of the motor home in Minneapolis.

CHAPTER 7

Ten hours later we reached the University of Minneapolis, as planned, to pick up Dr. Wineguard's assistants. Drowsy from the microwaved hot dogs that we had just stuffed ourselves with, we stepped onto the parking lot.

The answer to my second question slammed all of us wide awake.

"Tell us about the prehistoric monster!" Cameras clicked and whirred from all directions.

"Are you willing to stake your professional reputation on a legend?" A microphone almost bopped Dr. Wineguard's chin.

Someone grabbed my elbow and pulled me aside. A floodlight blinded me as she said, "Television Seven Evening News. Sondra Stevens reporting from the U of M science department. We're standing here with one of the computer whiz kids invited along on a million-dollar monster hunt. Tell me, what new technology are you bringing along to bag the monster?"

I opened my mouth to describe the Sonar Scanner, and instead of saying something incredibly intelligent expected from a computer whiz kid, I was punished for eating my last hot dog so fast.

"Eerrp," my stomach said directly into the camera.

I tried to recover quickly. "A Scooner Sanner. I mean, a

Sooner Sinner!" I became desperate. "A Sunny Skinner!"

The floodlight faded. "Come on, Mac," the newslady said with disgust. "Let's talk to the girl when she's finished with News Twelve."

"A Sonar Scanner!" I called to their backs. "A Sonar Scanner that amplifies sonar radar and converts the blips so that... aw, who wants to talk to you guys, anyway."

I wandered over as Lisa was finishing an interview. "... cameras can only work as deep as light can go, and of course to search for a monster as elusive as the Ogopogo we will have to go much beyond that depth. The Sonar Scanner then becomes the perfect surface-to-bottom research tool. Any further questions?"

Ralphy was saying to a newspaper journalist, "... revolutionary computer software as developed by Dr. Wineguard makes it possible for his scanner to show us everything beneath the surface as if the water did not exist between the boat and what is underneath..."

Dr. Wineguard was running his fingers through his hair and had coughed to clear his throat in front of another microphone. "This is a new era, where big business and science begin cooperation as they both seek mutual goals. In this case, Compudel has shown faith in my research and is about to be rewarded accordingly..."

I blinked as I stepped closer to Mike, whose voice reached me clearly. "... months and months of dedicated teamwork on our science project, and I couldn't have pulled it together in time for the win without a *little* help from my friends who—" he caught my stern frown and the silent cutting motion I made across my throat behind the interviewer's back "—all got the idea from the real computer whiz, Ralphy Zee," he finished meekly.

It was a media blitz and everyone seemed to have someone to interview, which left me with nothing to do except practice "Sonar Scanner, Sonar Scanner" as I wandered away from the action to sit on the steps below the motor home's side door.

Ten past seven, my watch read.

I sighed. Ten past seven. Ten hours and two restaurant stops closer to stepping into the boat that would search for Ogopogo.

I didn't know whether to be excited or impatient. Minneapolis to southern British Columbia meant traveling through the rest of Minnesota, entirely across North Dakota, Montana, and Idaho, and halfway through Washington State before turning north to enter Canada. That kind of distance seemed like forever.

And here I was, sitting alone and ignored while—for whatever reason—my friends were in the spotlight. I sighed again.

"Cheer up, kid." An almost whisper came softly from inside the motor home.

Every muscle in my body twitched in an instinctive jump response after years of Joel sneaking up. Then, as quickly, I relaxed. Joel was hundreds of miles away.

So I stood slowly and turned. And hung my jaw down to my feet.

The person who owned the voice continued. "It's only PR stuff. Mostly meaningless, but a grand kickoff like this is unfortunately necessary for our expedition. You aren't missing much by sitting here."

I gulped hard to pull my chin back up. "PR?"

"Public relations," she explained. "By the way, I'm Mel Waters, one of Dr. Wineguard's assistants."

"Mel?" It was hard at the moment to think clearly.

"Short for Melody." She smiled and I expected bells to chime.

Blond hair pulled straight back. Eyes like a clear Montana sky. An almost shy smile. She wore cotton slacks and a loose, fuzzy sweater. *Boy,* I thought, *why don't any of my schoolteachers look like this?*

"I hope I didn't startle you," she said. "I'm a scientific journalist, and I've been waiting quite some time for the chance to work with Dr. Wineguard. My luggage is back in the building, but I couldn't last another second before taking a look at his lab."

Why didn't Dr. Wineguard explain everything? "You haven't worked with him before?" I had to ask dumbly.

She shook her head. "Only James has, the computer assistant. I heard about this project in a science journal. It's like a dream come true that he accepted my application. It will let me complete my master's in journalism. With Dr. Wineguard, no less."

She stopped and grinned at her own enthusiasm.

"Journalism?" I asked.

"Sorry. I do carry on. I'm here to record everything for maximum publicity later. And to work with Dr. Wineguard. Wow! To finally see his portable lab. I never believed it would be this perfect. The computer power he has in here is staggering."

"So I'm told," I said. I made mental plans to start learning about computers from Ralphy.

Her beautiful voice again. "And he can take the lab anywhere he wants!" Suddenly she turned to face the computer lab, then faced me again. "Excuse me. Thought I heard something."

I smiled back. "Carry your gear?"

"That's a kind offer. Sure. It's back in the lobby of the science building." She stopped, puzzled. "I wonder why James hasn't shown up yet. He's already ten minutes late."

I was still in a half daze, making a note to myself not to let Mike or Ralphy know I was already three-quarters of the way into a major crush on this scientist.

"James?" I repeated.

She nodded. "The other assistant I mentioned. Actually, he looks a lot like my husband."

Wonderful. Hot dog burps, Sunny Skinners, and a crushed crush. What more could a guy ask for on the first day of an expedition?

CHAPTER 8

We were halfway through North Dakota the next day before James Bickley spoke his first words to us.

"Enough already of the newscast replays," he crabbed. "You'll wear out the VCR."

The night before he had merely grunted hello. During the few hours that we drove from Minneapolis after the media interviews, he didn't talk at all, let alone even give an explanation for why he had been late. Then not even a good-night before we checked into our own motel rooms late that evening in a small town close to the Minnesota border.

By then, of course, I at least had the explanation for why Dr. Wineguard and his sponsoring company, Compudel, were willing to pay for a team of inexperienced twelve-year-olds.

Publicity.

As Dr. Wineguard had explained with a wry grin after our stop in Minneapolis, publicity was worth money. The contest had promoted Compudel, even before promoting the trip itself. Yesterday a combination of school kids, world-famous scientist, and a one-million-dollar monster hunt had put Compudel in news stories all across the country.

Which is why we were watching ourselves on videos of

last night's news. Again and again.

"Ralphy, your hair stands out more than a flag," Mike had snorted. Our giggles to that remark were the last straw for James Bickley.

"Did you hear me?" he demanded. "No more noise!"

He was perched in front of a computer at the rear of the laboratory side of the motor home. He was short and wide, with a dark fierceness that reminded me of Dr. Frankenstein. His hair was thick and curled slightly, and he had a nose that looked as if it had been broken more than once. He seemed to have a permanent snarl on his face.

I sighed to look at Mel at the computer beside him. She was so nice and pretty and . . .

Lisa dug an elbow into my ribs. "Great scenery, huh?"

"Terrific, actually," I said without thinking.

She dug the elbow in deeper. "Outside, you dimwit. Snap your jaw back into place."

Before I could stop blushing, Dr. Wineguard called back over his shoulder from his position behind the steering wheel, "Who's hungry?"

Dumb question. When *weren't* Mike and Ralphy and I hungry?

Dr. Wineguard slowed as we approached the exit. The land had definitely changed now that we were past the green rolling hills of central Minnesota. The hills here were flatter and stretched longer. Trees grew in tight groups across the horizon. Grassland waved in the wind, and the sky, a drizzly gray the day before, was a pale blue in all directions.

This was our first break since leaving the motel at six this morning, and we were glad for the chance to stretch outside.

"Oops," Mel said as we started walking across the parking lot to the restaurant, "forgot my purse. I'll be right back."

"I'll wait for you," Lisa volunteered.

"No, no," Mel said quickly. "I'll catch up."

Our stacks of hot cakes had arrived before Mel made it to our table.

"It's about time," James grumbled.

Mel held up her purse and shook her head in flustered irritation. "I dropped it and change scattered everywhere. Finding all those coins nearly drove me nuts."

The rest of us shook our heads in sympathy with her. I noticed, though, her story didn't slow Mike or Ralphy down in their hot-cake consumption.

A half hour and two more orders of hot cakes later—I was surprised at how much I could eat, honest—we were ready to get on the road again.

"Backgammon?" Ralphy suggested when the pavement began rumbling beneath us.

"Nah," Mike said. He changed his voice to a whisper. "Newscast videos."

Ralphy's eyes widened, and he gestured toward James, who was busy at a computer screen.

"We'll keep the sound down," Mike whispered. "I want to watch the part where you notice that your zipper is undone."

Lisa rolled her eyeballs. Ralphy turned as red as he had on the newsclip. I tried to smother a laugh. It *would* be worth watching again.

Ever noticed that whenever you know you have to be super quiet, the smallest thing makes you want to giggle your brains out?

Without sound, the news stories had a different perspective, and we noticed new details. Lisa's arched eyebrows jumped up and down in synchronization with her moving lips. Mike scratched his head so often, it looked like he had lice. Ralphy, of course, cringed in horror halfway through as he realized his zipper was low, then squirmed for the rest of the clip.

Lisa grabbed my arm and pointed. Sure enough, in the background at one point, you could see me shuffling sadly away from the action.

There in the motor home, traveling down the interstate hundreds of miles from where the newsclips had been shot, we held our stomachs and rolled weakly as we tried to keep our own volume down.

Then I saw something flicker on the television screen.

I sat bolt upright, with not even a tremble of laughter left inside.

"Rewind!" I whispered. I did not want my imagination to be true.

"What?"

"Rewind! Rewind!"

They played it back, not understanding the wildness in my eyes.

I groaned. There it was, a flicker of movement to send chills down the back of any sane person.

"Stop it there. Back it up in slow motion."

Lisa noticed. She put her hand to her mouth.

"Great," I said aloud. "My call home can't even wait until supper today. My parents must be going crazy." I had promised to call home at the end of every day to let them know how things were going.

"Why?" Ralphy asked.

I frowned, clicked the video tape back a few notches, and pointed. "That's why."

Dimly, we could see two figures outlined in the rear window of the motor home as the camera panned it briefly. One of the figures—tiny and hanging upside down—did not particularly care about the fuss outside. The other figure, which was not a teddy bear, had its face glued against the glass in curiosity.

Mike groaned. "Joel."

I nodded, remembering how Mel had imagined a noise during our talk the day before. "None other. The little twerp must have stowed away."

Of all the ways to slow us down. A six-year-old as much ghost and conscience as brother was hidden somewhere in this motor home.

Sitting there, working up the nerve to tell Dr. Wineguard, I considered our options. None seemed good. I would probably have to be the one to escort Joel back to Jamesville. By bus, I guessed. There went my expedition.

It took getting mad about the unfairness of it to give me enough courage to finally go to the front of the motor home.

"Dr. Wineguard?"

He nodded without looking away from the road.

"Could we stop? I think my brother is here with us."

"The cute, polite one who doesn't say much?"

The one whose teddy bear I'd like to strangle.

I simply said, "Yes."

The hopeless tone of my voice must have convinced him more than my words, because he signaled to pull over immediately.

"On a replay of a news story," I said before Dr. Wineguard could ask his next question. "I saw him peeking out the back window. He must have hidden in one of the compartments beneath our seats. I'll bet Mom and Dad are going crazy looking for him back in Jamesville."

Dr. Wineguard's face made a subtle change as he focused on our problem. From angular and gawky, it became lean and intent, making me suddenly realize that most people would consider him handsome as he concentrated. He suddenly seemed bigger, more competent, not just a geeky scientist.

"And my cell phone's been on the blink. If they've been trying to reach you over the last hours..." He paused and shook his head in sympathy.

"We'll search," he said simply and gently. "When we find him, we'll decide what to do."

The motor home made a final lurch, then stopped.

All of us began pulling doors open and lifting seat cushions. It did not take long. I pulled the bench cover off the seat I had been using only minutes before, and there the little rat was.

Asleep with crusts of two sandwiches, a sprawled teddy bear, and no cares.

I wiggled a leg of his teddy bear.

Joel opened solemn eyes. "Hi, Ricky." He rubbed them and grinned sheepishly. "Let's pretend like this is a pirate story."

I groaned. I'd forgotten about the pirate stories I had read to him last week, full of buccaneers and stowaways finding adventure across the high seas.

"Come on out, Joel. Meet everyone before the two of us head back to Jamesville."

I wanted to be madder, but he was, after all, only a kid.

Just as I grabbed his arms to pull him from that cramped space, James Bickley shouted.

"Aaaaaagh!"

I whipped around, dropping Joel with a clunk.

James was clutching his throat and pointing frantically into another seat bench compartment.

"What is it?" Dr. Wineguard asked calmly.

James merely continued pointing as he turned white with horror.

Dr. Wineguard walked over. James bolted past Dr. Wineguard, slammed open the side door, and rushed out. The rest of us stayed exactly where we were.

"Hmmm," Dr. Wineguard said as he peered down. He reached in with both hands, fiddled briefly, then tugged.

When he straightened, the rest of us turned as white as James Bickley.

In his hand, Dr. Wineguard held a compact bundle of dynamite attached to a timer.

He spoke through a tight grin. "This certainly seems to be an explosive situation."

CHAPTER 9

Dr. Wineguard studied the bomb, then disconnected the wiring linking it to the timer. "Jonathan!" Mel said with an angry intake of breath. "What are you doing with that dynamite? How dare you play the macho man! Crazy fool, you could have killed yourself and the rest of us here."

He looked flustered for a moment.

Mel realized we were watching. "I'm sorry, Dr. Wineguard. I lost my head when I saw the dynamite. That was no way for a new assistant to act."

Joel tugged at my arm. "I need the bathroom."

That broke the tension.

"Poor rascal." I pointed where. "Over there. This time you won't have to sneak to it." I pictured him staying the night inside while we slept soundly in the motel. I grinned, then quickly wiped it from my face. Dr. Wineguard probably saw no humor in anything right now.

However, he chuckled. "Let's see, now. A stowaway, an assistant who thinks I'm a fool, and a bundle of dynamite. It's enough to make a fellow wish he hadn't quit smoking."

"Not quite," Mel said quickly.

Dr. Wineguard looked at her strangely. "Have no fear."

"Is everything okay?" A voice reached us from down the highway. Of course, James Bickley. He climbed aboard shortly after and listened to our discussion in sullen silence.

This was one grumpy, mean guy.

Less than two minutes had passed, but it seemed much longer. Somehow, with Dr. Wineguard so matter-of-fact about the dynamite he held, none of us were too frightened. Until the delayed reaction set in.

Dr. Wineguard moved to a seat on our side of the motor home and lowered himself gently.

Exhaustion and strain briefly crossed his face, and then came firm resolution. He thought aloud.

"All right, gang. We have two problems. Dynamite and Joel. At this point, I am beginning to suspect Joel might be the more dangerous of the two."

He smiled to show he was joking. Little did he know.

"He stowed away, but on the other hand, he also saved our lives."

I hadn't thought of *that.* If it weren't for the search for Joel, we would not have found the explosives.

I couldn't help blurting out my question. "For when is the timer set?"

Dr. Wineguard looked closer. "Eleven o'clock."

Less than a half hour away! I didn't know anything about explosives, but it wasn't hard to decide that there was enough in that bundle to totally destroy the entire vehicle. And us. It ruled out looking for any suspects on board the motor home.

"Who would want to kill us, sir?" Lisa asked. "Another computer company?"

"That's absurd," Dr. Wineguard snapped immediately. He shook his head. "Sorry, Lisa. I guess it's gotten to me, too."

"I know!" Mike slapped his thigh. "The people who will lose a million dollars when we find the Ogopogo. They could have snuck aboard last night and . . ."

Dr. Wineguard held up his hand. "One problem at a time. First, what do we do with Joel?"

"I guess I'll have to take him home by bus, sir. If you could lend me enough money, I can make sure you get repaid."

Joel clicked the bathroom door behind him, placed his hands on his hips, and said, "Nice pad."

Where he comes up with stuff like that, I'll never know. An old movie? Whatever the source, it cracked us up. All of us laughed away the fear that had been with us since finding the dynamite that Dr. Wineguard had already carefully disconnected from its timer.

Finally Dr. Wineguard wiped his eyes. "Ricky, if you agree to accept responsibility for him and can convince your parents to let Joel stay here, I'll make him a member of the expedition, too. After all, he did save our lives."

What a dilemma. Accepting responsibility for Joel was like accepting responsibility for a fox. On the other hand, to miss the expedition . . .

I smiled my widest smile and said through gritted teeth, "I'd love to have him along, sir."

"Then let's get on the road again."

That was it. Because Dr. Wineguard's cell phone wasn't working, I borrowed Mel's to call home. But it wasn't working, either. We had to wait until the next exit where I could use a pay phone. Mom was so relieved that Joel had been found, she didn't think twice before agreeing to seal my doom by giving him permission to stay.

The miles began blurring past us again. I spent ten or twelve of the next miles in silent prayer. Half, asking for God's help as I looked after Joel, the other half thanking God for sending Joel along in time to find the dynamite.

CHAPTER 10

It didn't occur to me until we were well into Canada to question Dr. Wineguard's reaction to the dynamite.

Why had he accepted the attempt on our lives so casually? If I were a scientist on an important mission, I wouldn't simply disconnect the timer from the bundle and continue as if nothing had happened. I'd be calling the police. I'd be demanding answers. *Who? Why?*

I hoped it was because he was trying to protect us from any worry.

I didn't spend as much time as I should have over that puzzle. By then we were all so excited to be in the Okanogan Valley of British Columbia that we could think of nothing else except the Ogopogo monster.

We had reached a lookout point near our final destination. We got out and stared in wonder at the view. "The monster was sighted just past that ridge in 1929!" Ralphy told us as he consulted his map. "A minister and two of his children were playing along the shore, and they watched it rolling in the water for nearly a half hour."

Below us, the town of Penticton lay nestled between the steep hills that sloped down to the lake-filled valley.

This is what I knew from Ralphy's excited discussions about the area over the last few days. The summer climate here was semiarid, similar to that of Southern California's coastline, and the valleys supported miles and miles of orchards.

Penticton itself was a tourist town. From May to September, its population was double what it was in the winter.

The town lay in the deep valley, with the rounded hills on each side climbing steeply into a hot blue sky. The distant line of land and horizon shimmered in the clear air.

North and south of Penticton, two lakes filled the valley bottoms. The one to the south, Skaha, was a short extension of Lake Okanogan, so that Penticton seemed to be on an ancient and huge land bridge between the two.

The other, Lake Okanogan, flung on the map like a necklace of glittering deep blue, lapped the base of the hills for another fifty miles north of Penticton. Along the entire stretch, it rarely widened more than a few miles. In fact, pioneer ranchers used to send teams of horses across the lake, guiding them from a rowboat in front as they swam. One of the Ogopogo sightings actually resulted from that. On a hot summer midafternoon in the early 1900s, we had read in an article, a rancher once saw both his powerfully swimming horses pulled straight down, to vanish without a trace.

I shivered as I looked down from the viewpoint. Ralphy had repeated and repeated one chilling fact: In some places, the lake was so deep that the bottom had not been measured.

Before I could worry any more about any of the hundreds of things that might go wrong on a boat in the middle of a bottomless lake while searching for a million-dollar monster—especially with Joel along—Dr. Wineguard interrupted our thoughts.

"What do you say, gang? Time to meet our boat captain and get ready for the first day of searching?"

All of us, except James Bickley and Mike, nodded. James was busy inside the motor home, fiercely attacking computer screens with those suspicious eyes of his and methodically clicking CDs between the computers as if they were slot machines.

Mike was concentrating equally fiercely but on something quite different.

Snap. Clinkle, clinkle, clinkle. "Nuts. I can't get any of these to—" He noticed our stares as we waited for him. Then he grinned. "A guy's gotta learn sometime. Especially if a girl can already do it."

A couple hundred miles earlier, at a rest stop, Mel had reached down to the pavement and picked up a bottle cap. She'd pressed her thumb and middle finger together, as if to snap her fingers, then tucked the edge of the bottle cap firmly between. With a quick upward tilt of her wrist, and a sharp snap of fingers, the cap had whizzed like a mini-Frisbee, shooting ahead sixty or eighty feet.

It wasn't something Mike wanted not to be able to do. At every stop after, he had taken his bottle cap collection outside, then practiced and practiced. Usually the bottle cap fell at his feet. One or two had actually whizzed briefly, enough encouragement to keep him trying.

He shrugged at our impatience. "Okay, okay, I'll admit the Ogopogo is more important than cap shooting." The unstoppable grin. "But not by much."

We climbed aboard. James, as usual, ignored us.

Dr. Wineguard shifted the idling engine into Drive. We began our final descent into the town of Penticton.

"Supper's ready!"

I tore myself from my daydream. In front of me, sitting like a heavy duck, was our boat for the expedition. It was a forty-four footer, once a pleasure cruiser. However, as our captain, Luke Stenson, had explained, the inside had been modified to make room for the extra equipment and bodies needed for a million-dollar chase.

He had told us a few more technical things about the boat, but I hardly remembered. Not only because my mind isn't built for that kind of information, but because Captain Luke Stenson's physical presence had such an impact it distracted me from his words.

He was a big man, but it wasn't his sheer size that overwhelmed. Nor the blond brush cut that made his head look like a friendly boulder chopped square across the top. It was the way he seemed put together, as if someone had tried packing eight hundred pounds of muscle where only two hundred pounds could fit.

I was glad he had a warm, lopsided grin as he spoke to us, because I would not have liked having him as an enemy. When he promised us that if anybody around knew the lake well enough to find the monster it was him, we believed it without a trace of doubt.

Of course, my daydream, while staring at the moored boat as it rode the slight swells, involved the touch-up details on how I managed to single-handedly capture the Ogopogo and then casually tell Lisa and Mel that it was nothing as they gazed at me with adoring eyes.

"Ricky! Your turn to serve."

I moved reluctantly away from the small strip of rough sand that made the beach. We were at the edge of an isolated peninsula roughly ten minutes' drive north of Penticton.

The motor home was parked near a stand of trees just behind us. Our camping area consisted of a fire pit and a weathered picnic table. The plan was to use the motor home as a day base and laboratory. It had the kitchen and computers. We were to use the boat during the day for search trips and at night, moored near the beach, as a place to sleep.

"Be right there!" I shouted back to Mel.

I walked by the picnic table. It had been set already. The others were making their way back as I entered the motor home.

Mel stood in the small kitchenette, stirring a large pot with vigor. James was in the back of the motor home, with a bowl of chili on the worktable in front of him.

"Hi," I said to him.

James ignored me.

"Don't worry about him," Mel said. "He cut his finger chopping some onions for me earlier, and it put him in a bad mood."

I noticed a bandage across one of his fingers.

She smiled at James. "See? Leave you alone in the kitchen for one minute and you damage yourself."

He didn't reply to her, either.

"Chili. Great!" I said to break the tension.

"Enough to feed an army." She pushed back a wisp of blond hair that had stuck to her forehead in the heat. "Can you take it outside for everyone?"

I accepted the potholders from Mel and struggled with the heavy pot.

Until stepping outside the motor home, I had almost forgotten about Joel. Not only had he been his usual invisible self, he had not innocently triggered any events, the ones which always get me in trouble.

I should have known better than to think it would last forever.

"I want to take a picture of the Ogopogo." His quiet voice came from nowhere. Not that I could see much with a huge pot between my arms.

"Ogopogo! It's here?!"

I was in the middle of feeling my way down the steps and hurrying to set the pot down so that I could grab my camera when I realized his voice had come from the steps. Not from beside the motor home. Not from under the motor home.

I also realized in that split second that Joel had daydreams of his own. And that he shared them with his teddy bear. By then it was too late. I had stepped on his shoulder.

With his yell of outrage and my yell of terror, we did a good enough job of attracting attention. Everyone at the picnic table saw how I twisted once to avoid landing on Joel, did a hop dance as my foot missed the step completely, and tottered briefly before slipping sideways. To fall on my rear end.

The pot banged my knee and tilted nearly upside down as I landed directly on my tailbone.

Hot chili spilled like lava down my shins and formed a thick puddle on the grass in front of my feet.

"Joooeelll!"

He smiled and tilted the pot upright. "See. Fixed."

"Thanks, pal." There was barely more than a bowlful in the bottom of the pan. The rest was already ant food.

James walked out of the trailer. He saw what Joel had done. "Idiot!" James shouted.

"Sorry," Joel said quietly.

"Joel didn't do it on purpose," Dr. Wineguard told James. "Besides, it looks like you already helped yourself. You won't go hungry."

James was holding that bowl of chili.

"Good thing," he said. "At least I'll have eaten." He pointed his bandaged finger at me. "You know I have too much work to do to sit around and wait for this kid to spill another batch."

"Certainly, James," Dr. Wineguard said calmly. "You go ahead. I'll start cooking again with Mel."

With a final glare at me, James stomped down to the picnic table and slopped down the last of his bowl of chili.

Dr. Wineguard stepped inside the motor home.

That left me and Joel.

I saw why he had been talking to his teddy bear.

"Is that my camera around your bear's neck?" I hissed.

Not that I needed the answer. My thirty-five millimeter camera with a zoom lens, the one that had taken six months of paper delivery to earn, was strapped to the dumb teddy bear.

Joel didn't have time to say a word.

James Bickley shrieked a horrible moan, then fell from the picnic table and began rolling on the ground in agony.

CHAPTER 11

It was an hour before Dr. Wineguard returned with Luke from their emergency trip to the hospital.

"Good thing you spilled that chili," Dr. Wineguard said to me with a brave smile as he stepped out of Luke's car. "Or all of us would have been just as sick as James. The doctor thinks bad hamburger triggered his attack."

I gulped. Our last sight of James Bickley had been of white-gray agony etched in sweat across his face.

"Bad hamburger?" Mel echoed. "I feel terrible. If only—"

Dr. Wineguard shook his head quickly. "Not another word. You can't be blamed for what happened."

Luke shook his head in dismay as he passed us on the way to the dock that held his boat. "A terrible sight, it was. No man should have to bear that much pain."

He left us in a brief silence broken only by the creaking of the dock under his weight.

"Wow!" Ralphy burst out when the lights of the boat flicked on as Luke made himself busy on board. "That's twice Joel has saved us. First the dynamite, then this chili."

Mike and Lisa nodded. Worse, Mel scooped Joel into her arms and hugged him close.

I groaned inside. Nobody seemed to be giving me a reward for nearly killing myself on those steps and dumping smoking hot chili all over my leg.

Dr. Wineguard stepped into the motor home, then stepped out almost immediately carrying a small duffle bag. "Ricky, I'll need you to come to the hospital with me." He seemed distracted, and he swung the bag back and forth as if he were lost in thought.

"Sir?"

It brought his eyes back into focus on us. "James may be staying there more than just tonight," Dr. Wineguard replied to my unspoken question. "He needs this gear delivered. And the doctor wants to look at your leg."

I grimaced bravely, hoping it would earn sympathy from Lisa or Mel. "I'd forgotten about it, sir. Especially how I'd made sure the whole pot landed on me instead of my poor little brother."

"He is worth saving, isn't he?" Dr. Wineguard said absently.

Lisa and Mel nodded vigorously at that comment. Joel smiled out from Mel's loving embrace.

Wonderful. I hobbled to the car anyway. Because if I put effort into it, I really could feel a bit of pain in one or two places.

Dr. Wineguard drove slowly and in deep silence.

The road we traveled wound its way around the base of the hills. Our headlights flashed occasionally off the lake, then back into the brush along the road. Twice we surprised deer into leaping away from the road.

Without warning, Dr. Wineguard snapped off the headlights.

For a moment we drove blind. Dr. Wineguard ignored my sharp intake of breath. "Beautiful, isn't it," he murmured. "The way God lights up the sky at night."

My eyes began to adjust. Although the lights of the town glowed miles ahead, the dark sky twinkled with the brilliance that stars show on clear nights away from a city.

I tried to make a joke. "Isn't that what people thought thousands of years ago? That it was God putting lights into the sky. I mean, as a scientist, you know better, right?"

"Ah yes," Dr. Wineguard said lightly. "The great god of science. Has it fooled you, too?"

"Fooled me?" I said. "Isn't science about what experiments show is true?"

"Hold that thought." Dr. Wineguard found the headlights again and drove for another hundred yards before stopping. He pulled off the road where it widened, then turned the ignition off.

"Come on outside," he invited.

We did so.

"Funny how that hobble disappeared," he noted.

I was glad for the darkness that hid my red face.

The engine made clicking noises as it cooled down. Slowly the insects resumed humming. The stars pierced the jet blackness above.

I leaned against the front fender and waited.

"Modern science definitely explores scientific truths," Dr. Wineguard began quietly from where he sat on the hood. "But sometimes it becomes a god in itself and often fools even those of us who believe in and search for God. After all, the fruits of science are all around us. Medicine, computers, knowledge. Even all the simpler things which make life so easy for us—cars, indoor plumbing, television—result from the scientific applications in research and inventions."

He paused again, this time for so long that I thought he had forgotten about me.

"All of these things are blessings for us. We now live decades longer than our ancestors of the Middle Ages. Our homes are marvels of comfort, even compared with the best that kings and queens enjoyed a hundred years ago. Yet, there is a danger in science."

He shifted to face me.

"The obvious danger is that we forget God, become distracted by all the wonderful things we discover, and forget that God still is behind them all. The other danger is less obvious."

It felt now as if he were thinking out loud. His voice was softer and carried clearly in the night air.

"Science, almost by definition, seeks 'how,'" he said. "It does not bother with 'why.' *How* do we make test-tube babies, *how* do we hook people up to machines to keep them alive longer, *how* do we make better weapons? We forget to ask why. *Why* make test-tube babies, *why* better weapons."

"But sometimes there are good reasons behind those—"

"And sometimes there aren't. My point is that we rarely ask beforehand, regardless if the reason is good or bad. Worse, those who are trained to ask 'why'—philosophers—are out of fashion these days."

I began to understand what he meant. "And another dangerous thing about science," I said. "It tries to prove the Bible wrong."

"What do you mean?" Voice still gentle.

"Like evolution and stuff. It's bad, isn't it, to let science go in those areas?"

Dr. Wineguard stood and faced me. "Ricky," he pleaded. "Please don't fall into that trap."

"Trap?"

"Don't undermine faith by trying to avoid questions you're scared it can't answer. Because our faith is strong enough for any doubts. It has been given to us by God, and it's survived and grown for thousands of years through hundreds of different cultures."

"First you tell me science is bad, then you tell me it's not. . . ."

"I've told you neither," he said firmly. "With science, we must not forget to ask 'why.' With our faith, we must not be scared to ask the 'how' in earthly things. That is why I am a scientist."

His statement made sense. "So it's okay to try fitting science into the Bible?" My confusion must have been obvious.

"Let me put it this way. If the Bible is a book of truths, whatever is truly true in science will also fit. The difficulties we face are in determining the truly true of science. Without forgetting to ask the—"

"The 'why'!"

He laughed, then continued. "During this week, it's appropriate in our search for a legendary monster that we try to answer some of those questions for you. Just remember this. It is much less important *how* God created our universe than *why*."

All of that was so much for me to think about that I almost forgave myself later for overlooking the things which were screaming out warning signals of danger.

Because when we arrived at the hospital, a nurse called Dr. Wineguard from the room that held James, and whispered urgently in his ear. She did not ask about my leg.

I couldn't hear anything of their discussion, though they were standing just outside the door. James was tossing in his sleep, his face still ghost white. The man in the bed next to James was sleeping, too, but with thundering snores. He was a huge man, and his right hand had flopped loose to drag on the floor. I noticed his ring scratching along the floor and thought it would be too bad if it got damaged, so I quietly moved closer and lifted his hand and arm onto his chest. The man's snoring did not change.

Dr. Wineguard motioned for me to leave the room with him.

"This is terrible," he said as the nurse left. "James was poisoned."

He caught me looking down at my leg. "Not a poison that could be absorbed through the skin. If you'd have had a cut and it could have entered your bloodstream directly, then the doctor would be worried about you."

"What do you mean, worried about me?"

"The poison was in the chili. James was the only one to eat from it. If you hadn't spilled it . . ."

It felt like the hallway rocked beneath me as I realized what that meant.

"You mean the whole pot could have, would have—"

"Exactly," Dr. Wineguard said. "Someone wanted all of us in here."

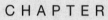

CHAPTER 12

"Don't be ridiculous, Ralphy. Boats don't have *steering* wheels."

In Jamesville the biggest body of water was the pond in the City Hall Park, and that—I did not want to remember—was barely big enough to hold a motor home. There, it didn't matter that Ralphy couldn't swim. Here, even on a boat as big as this forty-four footer, there would always be a life preserver in range for him.

Naturally, we had never before been on a boat as big as a forty-four footer, so I was prepared to forgive Ralphy for being dumb enough to assume it would have a steering wheel.

I said something to that effect. "In fact, Ralphy," I lectured as we walked onto the dock and prepared to step into the boat our first morning at the lake, "it's a different world on water."

We had spent the night sleeping in the cabins of the boat, but this was our first chance to really check it out. We'd gone back to the motor home for breakfast, and now we were finally ready to begin our search.

I thought of the pirate books I had been reading to Joel. "Port is left; starboard is right." I pictured the spoked wheels that pirates cranked in either direction. "Cars have steering wheels; boats have just 'wheels,' or 'the helm.'"

"Oh," he said as we stepped onto the deck of the boat.

I followed him onboard. We reached the helm and Ralphy pointed. "It sure *looks* like a steering wheel."

I hate it when I'm wrong.

Luke laughed at the shock on my face. It was a big man's laugh, full of chuckles and massive teeth, but warm enough so that I knew he was laughing *with* me, not *at* me. "The old-fashioned wheels aren't needed anymore. At one time, when cables were used to pull the rudder right or left, the wheel needed to be big enough to give leverage. Now"—he pointed underneath the console—"hydraulics do the work and manufacturers can install things that look exactly like the steering wheels of cars."

Sure enough, a tiny set of tubes disappeared in a mess of wires where he pointed.

"Oh." At least I knew that a rudder was the big paddle-like thing stuck in the water at the back of the boat. I shuffled back onto the deck before I said anything else stupid.

It was eight o'clock in the morning. The mists that had greeted us when we first stepped outside to stretch and yawn away our sleep in the cool early morning air had faded to be replaced by blue sky as far as we could see.

My sleep had not been the best. At Dr. Wineguard's request, I had not mentioned anything about the poison to anyone else. It was not something he wanted made public, so he had said he would tell Mel when it was appropriate and had left it at that.

Still, questions had tumbled through my mind over and over again. Who had tried to poison us? How? Why?

I could figure out nothing that made sense. Yet with the dynamite and poison, it was painfully obvious that somebody did not want this to be a dream vacation.

As Luke pulled away from the dock, I told myself that surely Dr. Wineguard knew what he was doing by remaining so quiet about all of it.

The bow crashed into small swells, and we rounded the peninsula to roar directly toward the middle of the lake.

South of us, about three miles away, was Penticton. North, the entire lake, in some places so deep no one knew where the bottom began.

I shivered, hoping it was from the wind and not fear.

Ahead, Luke pointed and yelled something that was lost to me in the noise of the wind and the slapping of waves.

I moved forward. "Pardon me?" I shouted.

"Those cliffs way north. That's where we're headed today. Wineguard—that is, *Doctor* Wineguard—has decided those will be the best places to give his scanner a trial run."

I nodded. Ralphy and Mike and Lisa were at the back of the boat, talking with Mel and Dr. Wineguard. James was not scheduled to be out of the hospital for a few days. Joel was on his back, almost lost in a huge orange life preserver, watching the sky with a smile of contentment.

Something about Luke's jacket caught my eye. Then I realized what it was.

"Hey!" I shouted and pointed at his jacket. "That emblem on your chest!"

It was a C-shaped lion's head in a full roar.

He smiled a neutral smile of not understanding.

"I saw a guy yesterday with one just like it." The guy in the hospital bed beside James. The one whose arm I'd lifted. His ring had matched the symbol.

"What?"

Oops. I suddenly remembered I wasn't that free to talk about the hospital. I pretended that it was hard enough to be heard without trying to explain the details and decided to only repeat myself. "I saw a guy yesterday with one just like it."

Luke nodded comprehension, then shook his head. "Impossible!" he shouted back. "It's a symbol from what you might call an academy. There are very few around."

I shrugged agreement, glad to be able to change the subject. Not that I cared extremely about finding out which academy he meant, anyway.

Joel stirred and came to stand beside me. He put his little hand in mine.

I hate it when he does that. It makes me remember how much I love the little turkey.

He remained patiently beside me the entire half hour it took us to reach the base of the cliffs.

They mounted the Sonar Scanner on a massive horizontal tripod that suspended it—facing down at the water—twenty feet from the side of the boat.

Insulated wires ran from the back of the "bazooka" along the tripod back to a computer beneath a sheltered canopy at the rear of the boat.

Dr. Wineguard stood there, fussing with switches and tapping his feet as he stared at the computer screen.

"I can hardly wait to see what the bottom looks like," I whispered to Ralphy.

He smiled patiently. "You'll have to wait until we get back," he said.

"But—"

"The computer here is simply set up to record the electronic information loaded onto it by the Scanner."

"But—"

"It takes an incredible amount of computer memory to reconstruct the images from digital information into a video stream of images. That's what home base at the motor home is for. The server there has the massive hardware necessary for the new program to convert everything to the television show you want so badly."

"So we won't see much here?"

"Not really."

"I knew that, of course."

Ralphy smiled. "Of course."

I frowned. "The monster could be right below us right now, and we wouldn't find out until back on land. That's not much good."

Ralphy shook his finger at me. "Don't jump to conclusions, Sherlock. We do see radarlike blips on the boat's screen. After we record the monster, at home base we'll be able to match those blips with what we see here on the screen. That way, when we are back on the water, we'll know immediately which blips match up to the Ogopogo."

I grinned. "I'm glad you're a computer geek, pal. Without you, I'd be lost."

Before Ralphy could reply to that, Lisa Higgins stopped by. Her hair was tied back, and she wore a T-shirt and denim shorts. The way she smiled against the sun with her tanned skin and white teeth made me glad just to watch. Between her and Mel, it made for some nice scenery. Not that I would admit it to Mike or Ralphy.

"Joel's getting restless," she announced. "And we both know how much trouble that could mean."

I nodded. "How about letting him listen to your Walkman, even if it is ancient?" Ralphy and I both snickered a bit.

"I told you before, I wanted to listen to old rock and roll. From my parents' cassette collection. Can I help it if they don't want to go digital?"

I shook my head.

"Apology accepted. Even if it was a good idea, I can't do it."

"I'll make sure he's gentle with it," I said.

"I'm not worried about that," Lisa said. "But I can't do it because it's not working. No matter what cassette I put in there, I just get hissing instead of music."

I shrugged. "Sorry to hear it."

She shrugged back. "Plenty of other things to do."

"Reading is never a bad idea," I said. "Maybe I can interest Joel in our newspaper clippings on the Ogopogo."

Lisa sent Joel over to us with Mike.

Ralphy dug into his pockets for our favorite clippings. As usual, I was happy to be wearing my sunglasses when faced with Mike's Hawaiian shirt.

Ralphy cleared his throat. "The million-dollar monster," he began. I closed my eyes to listen and bask in the warmth of the sun. All of us nearly had the clipping memorized. I could see it in my mind as Ralphy read.

Lake Okanogan is deep enough that when a boat sinks, even just a half mile offshore, it might be lost forever. Those count-less tons of blue, blue water make the mystery believable. *N'ha-a-itk.*

The lake monster. The Indians and early settlers called it N'ha-a-itk. Today, Canadians call it Ogopogo.

Imagine a snake longer than two city buses and as thick as a strong bear. That is Ogopogo. It has a horselike snout, flat tail, and the strength to break water with the speed of a powerboat.

On paper, it is hard to believe. But in light mist on calm water in quiet mountain air?

The first recorded sighting by a Caucasian took place in 1872. There have been vague and infrequent photographs since 1964.

Ogopogo has been attested to by unexcitable ranchers—some of whom lost horses to the beast—and even acknowledged by an Anglican minister. It was watched by some thirty cars of people in 1926, a group of eight people in 1984, and by two people in a boat on June 2, 1977. These two decided that discretion was much better than bravery, especially since they esti-mated the speed of the monster at thirty miles per hour. They left their bravery in their wake by heading the opposite direction at equal speed.

In all, there have been hundreds of eyewitness reports over the decades. Only definitive proof is lacking.

Photographs, good or bad, encourage the believers, but skeptics, of course, wait. The monster, like its counterpart, the Loch Ness monster of Scotland, must be captured to silence the scoffers.

Yes, Ogopogo in a zoo is a million-to-one long shot backed by local business owners (who have backed the offer with an insurance policy) who want to attract tourists. It places a one-million-dollar bounty on Ogopogo's head, payable when captured alive and verified by zoologists.

If and when the bounty is collected, cold science will finally end centuries of Canadian mystery and legend.

There was a careful rustling as Ralphy folded the paper and tucked it into his pocket.

No noise from Mike. Unusual, but considering we were about to begin the search of the century, not unexpected.

Cold science, I thought. *That's what it is. Cold science. Something that God lets us use for our benefit but that will never have the warmth and comfort of faith.* It was nice to know that some scientists, like Dr. Wineguard, easily fit science into God's world.

I smiled into the warm sun, my eyes still closed.

Then, startled, I opened my eyes abruptly to stare at the endless miles of blue water.

Captured alive?

This was supposed to be a million-dollar search, but I had not heard anything about Dr. Wineguard's having plans to capture it. I had not seen nets on board.

Surely the article was wrong. The Sonar Scanner video would be enough proof for the zoologists.

Or would it?

So far, none of us had been pressed into much action. I tried to shake off all my old doubts about the trip. With so little for us to do, why had they taken a gang of kids along? Who was trying to blow us up or poison us? What was with Dr. Wineguard's strange behavior?

"Action!" Dr. Wineguard shouted gleefully.

Can any man be that enthusiastic and be a fake? I asked myself. Then I resisted the temptation to smack my head. No man could be that well known as a scientist and be a fake.

My doubts faded as the first of the radar blips began their high-pitched beeping across the computer screen below the boat deck.

CHAPTER 13

At one point during our journey, somewhere in Montana, Dr. Wineguard had turned down the country tunes on the radio that were driving us nuts and explained he was about to tell us something very simple about expeditions.

"Ninety-nine percent sheer boredom, and one percent crazy excitement."

Then he had turned the song back up to leave us gaping like goldfish at the abrupt sentence that had come from nowhere.

By the middle of the second day on the lake, I understood. The trouble was, I had no idea how much of the ninety-nine percent we had covered and certainly had had no indication of what the one percent might be like.

All that had happened of any importance out on the lake the second day was that while Ralphy was busy looking at computers in the back of the boat, Mike and I were up front keeping Joel busy as we taught him how to spit properly.

I mean, you can't go through life with a kid brother who spits and lets it dribble down his chin.

At first, Joel could barely clear his chin. However, Mike and I were experts at getting a solid *wh-thppt*, and our distances away from the boat were encouraging enough for Joel to persist. Especially after he learned to clear his throat to get some heaviness into his spit.

Lisa did not appreciate our exhibition. She wandered up front once, looked at the tiny mess on Joel's shoes, and merely said "Gross" before flipping her hair back and leaving us glad we had at least wiped Joel's chin.

As we headed back after another day on the lake, our heads full of the meaningless blips that had hit us like dripping water all day, I finally voiced one of my doubts to Mike.

"You know," I said, "we don't seem to be doing much work around here."

He snorted. "Of course not. One, Ralphy's down there most of the time. And two, we're public relations stars. We don't need to work."

I thought for a second. "You *really* mean we're glorified pets kept on board to get them better media coverage."

Mike grinned. "Yup. But would you rather be at home?"

I thought for another second and grinned back. "Nope."

We were interrupted. *Wh-thppt!* Spray hit our faces, and it wasn't lake water skidding up from the bow of the boat.

We both stared at Joel, who was proud of his spitting display.

"Ricky," Mike said, "explain to Joel that he shouldn't face into the wind when he does that."

Three things happened that evening.

Mike snapped a bottle cap so hard that it stuck to the edge of the motor home door. James Bickley was waiting for us when we stepped off the dock. We had our first glimpse of the Ogopogo.

The most important of those three was something I hardly thought about until it was too late.

"Doc," James croaked through a strained face and almost-white lips immediately upon our return. "Have you run the blips on the home-base screen yet?"

"Not so fast, James. I'm more concerned about your health. Are you sure you should be here?"

"Very sure. No sense wasting money on a hospital."

Dr. Wineguard nodded, unconvinced. He politely moved to help Mel step off the deck, then counted the rest of us one by one as we passed him. "Lisa. Joel. Teddy bear. Ralphy. Mike. Nice shirt, by the way. Ricky. Luke. Me. All present and accounted for."

Finally he turned back to James. "Yes. We did run some of yesterday's stuff last night. What we saw was encouraging. The first test run showed everything down there as clear as day."

James scowled. "I hope it's the same tonight."

"Yes?" Dr. Wineguard asked mildly.

"Because when the taxi dropped me off here, the door to the motor home was unlocked."

"Unlocked?" Same mild tone.

"Yes. Unlocked. Anybody who wanted could have waltzed in and tampered with the computer. Hundreds of thousands of dollars of programming could be endangered."

Mel spoke quickly. "It . . . it could have been me. But I was sure I locked it behind me."

Mel had forgotten her binoculars somewhere in the motor home just after we had left shore in the morning. We had circled back quickly, and it had taken her only minutes to find them.

James turned his scowl on her. "That means it could have been open all day."

Mel's blue eyes shifted to the ground. "I suppose so. But I didn't mean . . ."

"Nothing stolen, James?" Dr. Wineguard interrupted.

"Not that I could see."

Such an optimist.

We all turned to walk to the motor home.

After grilled hamburgers, and before Dr. Wineguard had all the computers in place for our viewing of the day's run, Mike went back to his favorite activity: flicking bottle caps.

He was getting good at distance, but like Joel with spitting, his accuracy was dangerous.

I left Mike popping caps and retrieving them to pop them over and over again.

Inside the motor home, the computers were warming up.

I had seen the display the night before, and I knew it would fascinate me again.

In the background, a humming of five computers linked for massive power. A gradual lightening of the primary monitor screen.

Then the muted blips that we had heard during the day, except in quicker sequence. As the screen brightened, fuzzy lines sharpened to form outlines, then solid shapes.

As the blips quickened more and more, the shapes became easily identified, and it was as if we were panning the lake bottom with a close-up television camera.

The craggy rocks looked no different than the sides of the hills. The vegetation was not the same, of course, but the television screen showed us everything, just as if the water were not there.

I held my breath. The night before, I had held it in curiosity. Now it was in anticipation. A show like this made the entire day worthwhile.

The night before, Dr. Wineguard had fast-forwarded the blips, concentrating hard for the patterns that showed movement in the water. Whenever he had stopped, we had seen fish of all sizes but not the Ogopogo.

This time, I watched and felt a visible thrill as the fuzzy lines appeared on the screen. We were here! The gang of us from Jamesville was actually here, with the chance to become part of history. If it turned out to be the Ogopogo . . .

It was a moment to say a silent prayer of thanks, the ones you use when you have a warm glow of happiness that seems to hug you. Dad once told me those are the times that God especially likes to know you are thinking of Him and what He gives to us.

The glow of happiness stayed warmly fuzzy inside me, just as fuzzy as the lines on the screen.

"Strange," Dr. Wineguard muttered to the line of us—Ralphy, Lisa, me, and Mel—all leaning forward. Last seen, Joel was practicing his stuff right alongside Mike. "It should be clearing up right now."

It didn't.

The blips quickened and outlines of rock and fish appeared, but they remained unfocused.

"Hmmm." Dr. Wineguard began to adjust controls on the computers as he let the blips continue. "This *should* be fixable."

Clink. "Ooops."

Mike had hit the side of the motor home.

I frowned and stood quickly. It was not a good time for Mike to be interrupting with something as silly as bottle-cap shooting.

I reached the doorway.

"Hey," Mike hissed as he reached it at the same time. "I stuck it!"

"Good one."

"No, really," he insisted. "I snapped so hard I buried it into the edge of the doorway."

I looked closer. The bottle cap *was* stuck into the doorframe.

"No way," I said and gave it a yank.

It pulled loose easily.

"Strange," I echoed Dr. Wineguard's earlier words quietly. "This seems to be—" I held the cap close to the frame again. It jumped as if pulled, right to the frame—"magnetic."

I yanked it away again, then teased it closer until, sure enough, the cap jumped into place, just as surely as metal to a magnet.

"Why on earth would—"

"Whooo-eeee!" Mel's triumphant shout nearly burst me from my skin. "It's a monster!"

Mike and I looked at each other.

"A monster?" we said at the same time.

We spun quickly to see the monitor screen.

Dr. Wineguard reversed and then advanced the blips. "It may be exactly that," he said without emotion.

We saw a huge, dark shape move into view, then out.

"How could it not be?" Mel almost squealed with delight. "Did you see the size of it?"

Dr. Wineguard grimaced. "Until I get this focus thing licked, we can't be sure of anything. I don't think it's a problem with the server's hard drive."

He pointed at the computer attached to the monitor. "In there. And until we get this problem solved, no Ogopogo."

CHAPTER 14

The good about the next morning was that I could have a restaurant breakfast instead of campfire cooking in front of the motor home. The bad was that James Bickley was with me.

All because of a conversation the night before.

"I insist I be the one to take the computer in," James had told all of us when it became apparent that the problem of focus was a serious one. "I'm not well enough to go out on the lake, so I might as well go into town."

Outside, it was dark and quiet. The rest of us were dancing on the edge of our seats in excitement from seeing the Ogopogo deep in the cold waters of Lake Okanogan.

"Can I go along to get souvenirs?" Joel had piped up.

"Why not?" Dr. Wineguard said after a pause. "James?"

"I didn't hire on as a baby-sitter."

"Sir," I said quickly to Dr. Wineguard, "it may not be such a good idea. Joel has a habit of, um, disappearing."

Another short pause. "Okay, Ricky. Why don't you go instead. Buy us some postcards and trinkets while James works on the faulty hard drive."

Wonderful. Me and my big mouth. Joel and his bad habits. Both meant that if during day three they ran into the blips we thought were the Ogopogo, I wouldn't be around. No, I would be stuck with James on land.

Then, as everyone had gotten ready to make their way back to the boat to sleep for the night, Dr. Wineguard had pulled me aside and whispered something that was still on my mind as I finished mopping egg off my plate with the pancake on the end of my fork.

He had said sternly, "Don't go near the computer store. Understand? Shop for souvenirs. Wander town. But when you're finished, wait for James at the car."

What was that about? I wondered again. *What does Dr. Wineguard know about the danger of the situation that—*

"How much are you going to eat, kid?"

"Mmmpphh?" Lost in my thoughts about the night before, I nearly choked with surprise.

James repeated himself. "I said, you going to leave any food in this restaurant?"

"Good one, sir."

I think he was unhappy because he couldn't eat much due to the lingering effects of the food poisoning. His skin was still whiter than the belly of a dead fish, and he had barely sipped on his coffee.

He ignored me and started reaching for money, which meant I had to finish my fourth plate quickly. Could I help it that the restaurant had an all-you-can-eat special on pancakes?

CHAPTER 15

The rest of my day did not get off to a good start.

As I stood outside the restaurant, waiting for James to pay, I noticed, above the entrance to a pharmacy, one of those electronic signs that display the temperature, time of day, and advertising.

Twenty-eight?!

"Excuse me, ma'am," I said to a fat lady who squeezed through the pharmacy door and jiggled her way down the sidewalk toward me. It took a moment for all of her to stop. She stared down her jelly-bean nose.

"Do you find it cold?" I smirked at my humor.

"Eh?"

"I mean, if it's *really* twenty-eight degrees, we'd better get our coats." I pointed at the sign, which had obviously gone bonkers.

"You're American, eh," she sniffed.

How did she know? I nodded.

"Thought as much. We use Celsius here."

"Celsius. I see." Not seeing at all.

"Celsius degrees," she explained without patience. "Not Fahrenheit."

"Oh."

"And if you're trying to be smart about my husband's drugstore sign . . ."

James rescued me by coming through the restaurant doors. That's when I should have known it would be a lousy day. When I had to be rescued by a grump like him.

"Spare a quarter, sir?" I asked quickly to change the subject.

"Get real and quit wasting time," James said.

The lady gasped at both of us and walked away.

James placed his hands on his hips and surveyed the street. Whatever he was looking for did not appear. He finally spoke.

"The computer shop is called"—James grimaced—"*Mac* nificents. Get it? *Mac*nificents."

"Oh," I said with wide eyes. "You mean Mac from Macintosh computers."

He nodded with satisfaction. Some grown-ups never catch sarcasm.

"I'll be there a while," he said. "No way am I letting somebody from a rinky-dink town mess with it unless I'm supervising."

"Meet you at your car?"

He consulted his watch. "In five hours. Don't get in trouble."

I was almost disappointed. What, on top of all the other things slightly odd about this trip, could be the harm in stopping by the computer shop? But there were the whispered instructions from Dr. Wineguard the night before. So I looked for a bookstore.

Glad to be alone, I searched and found a secondhand bookstore and ran across a book I had always wanted to read. It was by a guy named Bill Myers, who wrote really funny stuff. That done, I wasted as little time as possible picking up souvenirs, then headed for a quiet spot to read.

Penticton's downtown was just south of the end of Lake Oka-nogan. I had only four or five blocks of strolling in the morning sun to hit the beach. I found a spot in the shade and settled in for an enjoyable wait.

Time whizzed by as it does when you get inside a good book.

I laughed in places, then turned red when I noticed people on the beach staring at the sounds coming from me, something I forget about while reading.

Then, too soon, it was time to go.

I got to the car. James was not waiting for me.

So I leaned against the bumper and read more. Shifted as my legs got sore, sat on the hood, and read more. And more. Then I realized it was at least an hour past our meeting time.

Great.

Maybe repairs were taking longer than expected. I waited another half hour.

Then it dawned on me. With the way this expedition was going, the explanation was probably not good. James could have had a relapse. Or, worse, with all the weird stuff that had happened—a dynamiting, then a poisoning—maybe James was in trouble.

Call the cops?

I shook my head as I thought. No. What could I say to them? Excuse me, sirs, I have a hunch. Please follow me on a wild-goose chase.

Then a terrible thought hit me. I had assumed Dr. Wineguard wanted me away from the store for *my* safety. *What if Dr. Wineguard is actually trying to hide something?*

I thought long and hard and waited another ten minutes.

Then I went to a phone booth and looked up the address for Macnificents.

The shop was down a quiet side street, away from the bigger department stores and office buildings.

The sun, still strong and hot, was casting the longer shadows of late afternoon as I slowly moved to the front of the store.

Nuts. The windows had shades. Closed. That should have told me something.

I tried the front door and then pushed it open, surprised it wasn't locked.

The showroom area was dark. Computer terminals and displays were silent. I nearly jumped at the sight of a figure looming huge from the shadows.

Idiot, I told myself. It was only one of those life-size cutout cardboard displays.

Funny, I then thought. *Not even five o'clock. Where's a staff person? Why are the lights off?*

A small, short hallway at the rear of the showroom showed a gleam of brightness.

"Hello?" I called to anyone in the work area back there.

No reply.

I should have known better. After all, it was an open store, with thousands of dollars of equipment, and nobody around. But I was too preoccupied to think of it that way.

I stepped forward.

A shadow detached itself from the cardboard display cutout.

Before I could react or even cry out, something crashed against the side of my head.

Later—I think much later—there was the sound of someone groaning. I finally realized the groans were coming from me, that it was my head and body on the cold, hard floor. Then the blackness gently took me away again.

CHAPTER 16

"... James is becoming too much trouble."

"You're right. Maybe we should do something about it."

In my crazy dream, the voices belonged to Mel Waters and Captain Luke. The dream continued but I couldn't see the faces.

"But getting rid of him will cause too much suspicion," said the soft voice that sounded like Mel's.

"I almost don't care. But listen—" The voice stopped, then began again. "We'll talk later. I don't want Wineguard to see us discussing this, and he'll be here any minute."

Black silence and a floating drift through nothing. Another dream began. This time Joel was pointing to the timer on a bundle of dynamite. I could see his lips move but heard nothing.

What was wrong with me? I shook my head in frustration.

Mistake. Major mistake.

Beams of pain echoed through my skull. In my dream, I groaned.

"He's awake!"

Awake? Who?

I twisted, curious to know who they meant, and more pain throbbed. Dimly, a hospital smell pinched my nose. Then came the quiet clicking of footsteps down long corridors.

It took great effort, but my eyes fluttered open.

"Yes, he is awake! Can you hear me, Ricky?"

It was Mel, leaning over me, the soft touch of her hand against my forehead. Crowded behind her, Dr. Wineguard peered over her shoulder.

"Can you hear us, Ricky?" This time it was Dr. Wineguard who asked.

I tried to croak a reply. "What time is it?"

"I'll get the nurse." Mel left the room with a rapid swish of her slacks.

"Ten at night. You'll be okay," Dr. Wineguard said to me. "Just as the doctor promised us. No concussion, but you'll have a terrible headache."

I already knew about the headache part.

"James? Ogopogo?" Somehow, I could not make complete sentences.

He smiled. "James is fine, too. He's the one who found you. As for the Ogopogo..."

A square-shouldered, surly woman in starched white marched into the room. Mel followed discreetly.

"Ogopogo," the nurse snorted. "The boy has had enough excitement."

Mel saw how I struggled to sit.

"No Ogopogo," she said quickly. "James is back at camp. He ran the computer while we waited here. What we hoped was the monster was only a sturgeon."

I sat back. "Stir?"

The nurse moved to my bedside and placed a pill under my tongue. Mel answered as the nurse tilted my head back and poured some water. Even gulping shot pain in all directions.

"Fresh-water sturgeon," she repeated. "A slow-moving fish that can weigh up to several hundred pounds."

"Oh." Her face began to swim in front of me.

In the fog that moved in, I began to remember more, and I fought again to sit up. "Store. Hit me."

"Shhh," Mel whispered as she placed a cool hand on my forehead. "We'll talk about it in the morning."

"Morning." My tongue felt thick as I tried to speak.

"Let him sleep," the nurse said. "Give him a good night's rest, and he'll be as good as new."

I giggled as her face dissolved, but no sound came out as the light faded on me.

The nurse had lied. In the morning I was not as good as new. Angry locomotives rumbled through my skull each time I turned my head.

But it was worth it for the sympathy showered on me by Mel and Lisa as I arrived at the motor home.

I winced manfully as I stumbled from Luke's car to greet everyone.

"Let me help you," Lisa called.

"I'll . . . I'll be fine," I said with enough of a tremor to get immediate concern from her.

She led me to the picnic table and helped me sit.

Mel appeared with some damp cloths.

"How are you feeling now?" she asked.

I smiled bravely.

They both began gently applying the cool cloths.

"Seven stitches," I whispered. "It's nothing."

Mike and Ralphy, who knew as many tricks as I did about getting sympathy, or cookies, from females, shot me dirty looks from the open doorway of the motor home. Joel, the little rat, didn't seem concerned one way or the other. Dr. Wineguard, Luke, and James were already at the boat.

In the warmth of the early morning sun, the day before seemed like it had never happened. But I still had questions.

"Yesterday," I began. "What happened at the computer shop? Was it robbed? Where was James? What did—"

Mel put up a hand to stop my questions. "Attempted robbery. The police have decided that the thief entered the store just before closing, that is, shortly before five. You must have gotten in just after he shut the lights off to make it look closed."

I nodded. Slowly. Looking for sympathy or not, it still hurt.

"They figure he must have been just about to go into the back when you interrupted. He bashed you and ran out."

"Why?" Lisa asked. "Why not just run?"

"Probably because he didn't want to be identified."

Identified! That word jolted me and suddenly I knew I had not been dreaming in the hospital. Those voices *had* belonged to Mel and Luke. That meant there had been a desperate reason the thief or thieves did not want to be identified.

Mel continued, unaware of the sick thud in my stomach. "James couldn't find Ricky at the car. He was backtracking and walked back into the computer store just as the owner came out from the back. They both found him there on the floor."

The gray chill that hit me was not from my headache, and even the sun could not warm it away. What had I heard?

"Are you okay, Ricky?"

"Yes," I mumbled as I recalled the words. "*. . . James is becoming too much trouble . . . but getting rid of him will cause too much suspicion.*"

I groaned, and not from the headache. Lisa squeezed my hand.

Suddenly too many things were much too clear.

"Maybe you should stay off the boat today," Mel was saying.

I wanted to shake her by the shoulders and demand answers.

Instead, I forced my voice to be steady.

"I think the fresh air will do me good." Not only that, but I needed to talk to Mike and Ralphy.

I made a promise to myself never to fall for a pretty face again.

CHAPTER 17

Three hours later we were in the middle of the lake. The constant below-deck beeping of the Sonar Scanner was not pleasant for someone with seven stitches above his left ear, nor was Joel's odd spitting attempt as he improved his distances.

Just before getting on the boat for the day, I had examined the stitches with the help of Lisa's pocket mirror. All seven stitches were tight together, almost in a semicircle, where something had cut deeply into my scalp. I had not looked again.

To this point, Mike and Ralphy thought I had remained so silent at the front of the boat because of a headache.

They were only partly right. What nagged at me was wondering why I had dreamed about the timer, why Joel had pointed at it. What hurt me worse than the headache was replaying those words I had heard in the hospital.

Not even the beauty of the far-off hills cutting sharply against the sky cheered me. I was desperately trying to arrange any pattern of events that did not point to Mel being guilty.

I found none.

Then the nagging quit as I realized what my subconscious had been trying to tell me about the timer. I could delay my talk with Mike no longer. With a small grunt of pain, I swung to my feet from my position at the bow, rolling with the slight pitching of the boat as I moved back to call for Mike.

Ralphy, I knew, would not come out. He had the computer to occupy him. Lisa I did not want in on this. And Joel had spitting to practice.

I caught Mike's eye with a slow wave of my hand. Even that much effort hurt. He joined me at the front of the boat.

"When you landed yesterday, did anyone leave?"

"Leave?"

"Yes," I said crossly. "Go away, depart, get in a car and go. That sort of leave."

"Boy," he said, "I'm glad you don't get hit across the head every day."

"Mike!" It came out with a hiss that made me realize how badly I wanted him to prove me wrong. "Did Mel leave the base yesterday afternoon?"

He thought for several seconds. "As a matter of fact, she did. With Luke, in his car."

"Mike, this is important. What time did they leave?"

He frowned in thought. "Four o'clock. I remember because I was so hungry that . . ."

I didn't hear the rest. Four o'clock was plenty of time to get to Penticton to try to ambush James. Instead, I had blundered in.

Whatever Mel and Captain Luke had planned, I had gotten in the way.

My face must have showed my thoughts. "Hang on, buddy," Mike said. "You're not thinking . . ."

I was thinking exactly that. I sighed as all the clues fit into place. "Let's start from the beginning," I said. "Tell me, what time was that dynamite set to go off?"

"Eleven o'clock," Mike answered. "Barely a half hour after we found it."

"Or so we thought."

Mike lifted his Yankees ball cap and scratched at his red hair. "You're telling me different?"

"Much different. We thought then none of our group would have done it because, of course, he or she would have been in as much trouble as the rest of us when the dynamite blew."

He nodded.

I dropped my first bomb. "What if the timer was set for eleven o'clock that *night*?"

Mike slowly jammed his cap back into place and stared at me with thoughtful eyes.

I continued with a rush. "Tell me one other thing. Who stayed in the motor home that night and worked while the rest of us slept in a motel?"

"James. But we thought nothing of it at the time."

"Exactly. That means when the dynamite blew, only he would have been . . ."

"Hang on, pal. You're not suggesting . . . "

I took a deep breath. Now that I was saying it aloud, I realized how true it must be.

"I'm saying it was Mel who stayed behind while we were in the restaurant that morning. She told us she had dropped her purse, but it gave her enough time to plant the dynamite. She set the timer for eleven at *night* to get rid of James."

I continued in a rush. "I'm saying it was Mel who poisoned the chili that sent James to the hospital. She was the one who made it."

"Poison!"

"Yes," I said firmly. "Poison. Dr. Wineguard wanted it a secret, didn't want any bad publicity. And I'm also saying she's the one who went back, alone, from the boat, and who also admitted she was the one who had left the door open all day."

I moved to the edge of the boat and stared at the water as I told Mike about what I had heard in the hospital.

"And finally, Mike, I'm saying it was Mel or Luke who bashed me over the head in the computer store."

We sat in silence for several minutes. The distant cry of sea gulls seemed haunting. Only a day earlier, those same cries had seemed like laughter.

"Okay," Mike said. "Maybe they want James gone. Why?"

"Besides the fact that he's a miserable grump?" That, at least, earned a grin.

"Besides that," Mike said. "Why?"

"I wish I knew. I wish I knew a lot of things. Why Mel? What's the connection between her and Captain Luke?" I shrugged helplessly. "We know a lot but we know nothing, know what I mean?"

Behind us, the constant beeping of the Sonar Scanner made a weird melody.

Mike spoke quietly. "We'll get all the answers as soon as we figure out one thing."

I waited.

"What's in it for them?" he asked. "How do they profit with James out of the way?"

A million-dollar question, and I didn't realize it at the time.

CHAPTER  18

That night Dr. Wineguard smoked his first cigarette in seven years.

"There is no possible way for the scanner playback to be this unreliable," he said. His eyes blazed with the first traces of anger I had seen him show.

"First the computer hard drive. Now the program itself." He left his cigarette in his fingers as he waved his hand.

Then he realized he was smoking. "Filthy habit. I should never have bought an emergency pack. These problems have got me so upset, I don't even know what I'm doing."

He threw the cigarette onto the ground and stamped all of his anger into it.

When he looked up, there was his quiet smile again.

"Glad that's out of my system," he said. "Time to roll up my sleeves and fix the software. I think it means going right back to unlocking the master."

He grinned sheepishly, then entered the motor home. That left Mike, Ralphy, Lisa, and me outside.

Only a few minutes earlier, Dr. Wineguard had tried playing back the day's scanning. The screen had not warmed up; it had remained blank while the sound track continued.

"Explain to me," I asked Ralphy quietly. "Software and hardware."

"No problem," he replied. A trace of mustard lined the left side of his mouth. It didn't seem to be the time to remind him that napkins are a good idea after hot dogs.

"Hardware makes up the actual pieces of the computer system. There is a monitor—the screen—a keyboard for inputting data, a mouse, and most important of all, the hard drive. It stores all the information. That's the piece, as you know, that James took into town for repairs."

"Software? Unlocking the master?"

"No problem again. Software is the program used by the hardware."

Lisa nodded. "I get it. Hardware is like the brain itself. Software is like the thoughts used by the brain."

Ralphy grinned with delight. "Exactly. Except instead of thoughts, the software programs are stored digitally on CDs. They used to be recorded with magnetic impulses on disks or sometimes on tapes."

"What's this about a master program and unlocking it, Ralphy?"

"Security issues, because computer information can be changed or copied too easily."

"Copied? Too easily?" Out of the corner of my eye, I watched Joel. Just because we were relaxing on a warm, starlit evening didn't mean I could forget about him completely. It helped, though, that his teddy bear was tied to the picnic table. Since Joel wouldn't go anywhere without his teddy bear, I was safe for a while.

"Oh yes. Copied. I'm probably telling you something you already know, but a single CD can hold thousands of pages of information."

I nodded.

"Copying that information onto another disk or onto a backup tape takes only minutes."

"Hang on," Mike protested. He was rolling a bottle cap in his fingers. "What's the difference between a program and information?"

Ralphy beamed. He obviously enjoyed being an expert. "A program is a set of instructions to the computer. The information is the result of those instructions being put to use."

"I see," Mike said absently. He snapped, and the bottle cap whizzed into the blackness.

Something began bothering me. Something important had just happened. What was it?

I frowned.

Ralphy misinterpreted my frown. "Sorry, Ricky," he said. "Getting back to your question about unlocking the master program. You know that part of the key to Dr. Wineguard's Sonar Scanner is the computer translation of sonar blips into graphics that appear identical to television."

I nodded again, glad my head hurt much less than it had earlier in the day.

"That translation is done with a unique and very complex program. At this point, it is the only one of its kind in the world. That's why Compudel is so willing to sponsor this expedition. Publicity and a trial run at the same time. Once Dr. Wineguard proves the program works, they can sell it for major dollars."

This time Lisa frowned. "But if it can be copied so easily, why would people pay for it? I mean, maybe the program was hard to develop, but each copy only costs as much as the CD or whatever is used to hold the information."

"Hah!" Ralphy crowed. "That's why the master program has a lock built into it. You're a hundred percent right. You see, programs aren't like, say, new cars. The first prototype of a car costs millions to develop, but each new car still needs to be built like it. Programs might cost as much to develop originally, but they are so easy to copy that they have to be protected. This program—"

"How does the lock thing work?" My voice must have sounded impatient. Only because of the persistent nagging at the back of my head. I almost wished for the old headache instead. Almost.

"Okay," Ralphy whispered. "We'll go inside and you can see."

We followed him into the motor home, but not before I double-checked to see that Joel was still patiently baby-sitting his teddy bear.

Hunched over the main computer screen were the three of them: Mel, James, and Dr. Wineguard.

"He won't let you see much," Ralphy continued whispering. "But if my guess is right, he's just about to punch in an access code."

"Access code?"

"Security code. The password telling the computer it's all right to release or alter the original program. At this point, it can be copied or tinkered with."

"James," Dr. Wineguard said with a voice absent in concentration. "You should step away."

James did so.

Dr. Wineguard started slowly pushing keys.

"Security issue," Ralphy said. "Dr. Wineguard's the only one who knows how to access it."

"It seems to be a long code," I said.

"Yup," Ralphy answered. "You'd make it that long, too, if you knew the program was worth millions."

Whatever was still plucking at me immediately disappeared. *Millions?*

It felt like the motor home was shifting under my feet. I had to breathe quickly to get air. *Millions! That was it!*

Another thought, very disturbing, hit me in quick succession. In his total concentration, Dr. Wineguard had forgotten to ask Mel to back away from the screen as he entered the code. As if he trusted her but not James. By the scowl on James's face, he'd noticed, too.

"We have to get outside," I hissed. "Now!"

I backed away, nearly stumbling in my anxiousness. Fortunately, Mel and James and Dr. Wineguard were so engrossed with the computer they did not notice.

When the rest of us were gathered near the picnic table, I tried to calm myself.

"What is it, Ricky?" Lisa asked. Her eyes grew wide. The near panic must have been obvious on my face.

"Something much too big is happening around here. And Mel and Dr. Wineguard and Captain Luke are all in on it."

"Come on." Ralphy half laughed. Dr. Wineguard was his hero.

Above the thumping of my heart, I explained everything Mike and I had already talked about.

They stared at me.

Mike said, "So what's the big development that's got you sweating?"

"What did you tell me this afternoon?"

"That Joel couldn't spit past his chin even with a good wind at his back."

"Mike!"

"I told you," he said, "that we had to figure out what was in it for Mel and Captain Luke. I didn't say anything about Dr. Wineguard."

I turned. "Ralphy, how much did you say that program was worth?"

"Millions. Even the military would be interested in something like that."

"Don't you get it, Mike? The Ogopogo is nothing compared to the program itself. Mel and Captain Luke want the program, and James is in their way."

"Why isn't Dr. Wineguard in the way?" Lisa asked.

"That's the worst of it," I said slowly. "He's in on it, too."

I lowered my voice. "We knew from the beginning that James is a Compudel employee. He's not Mr. Manners by any means, but he works hard for them. Day and night he's at the computers."

"That's not telling us anything new," Mike snorted. "Especially the part about Mr. Manners."

"Wineguard isn't exactly a Compudel employee. He just uses

their research money for a highly secret program, so secret he won't let James know the master access code."

"Hey," Ralphy protested. "It doesn't mean Dr. Wineguard's in on a plot to steal the program."

"Look," I said. "If they wanted to get rid of James, why not monkey with one of the other computers and send him into town to get it fixed? They'd know exactly when and where to find him. That would explain why Mel and Captain Luke went into town. It was bad luck for them that I happened to be at the shop. Especially since . . ."

I paused, remembering how Dr. Wineguard had specifically told me to stay away. He could have had only one reason for that. I didn't want to say it, but I had to. First I told them about the warning Dr. Wineguard had given me regarding the computer store. He, too, must have known Mel and Captain Luke would be going there and hadn't wanted me to get hurt. And if that wasn't enough proof, I told them the clincher.

"Think, Ralphy. Dr. Wineguard told only James to back away from the computer as he entered the access code. Not Mel. Obviously, they're together on this. I'd guess that somehow Dr. Wineguard wants Mel and Luke to steal the program so they can split the money later."

Ralphy dropped his eyes to stare at the ground. Lisa shivered. Mike whistled sharply.

If I was right, we were smack in the middle of a nest of human vipers.

CHAPTER 19

Mike, Ralphy, Lisa, and I had all agreed to pretend everything was normal while we waited for enough proof to take to the local police. So early the next morning, all of us went out on the boat as if nothing were out of the ordinary.

The boat had left slowly, as if Captain Luke were afraid to make noise in the eerie calm of the mist that had settled heavily on the lake.

In the gray mist it was easy to wonder about an Ogopogo monster and shiver. Trees on the shoreline rose and fell like ghosts as we slowly cruised along the side of the lake. All sound died. Even the hissing and sputtering of the boat's twin engines was muted. We each clung to the metal railing of the boat, and one by one stared silently in thought at the passing mists.

My thoughts jumped back to the night before. Something Ralphy had said about magnetic computer information had bothered me.

I closed my eyes. We had been talking. Mike had grinned, placed a bottle cap between his fingers, and—

That's it!

The magnetic doorframe. A strong enough magnet that Mike had once flicked a bottle cap that stuck to it. It *must* have something to do with all of this.

I moved closer to Ralphy. He, at least, would have an answer.

"Ralphy," I whispered in the hush around us. "You said something last night about information stored magnetically."

He nodded slowly. I could tell by the tightness of his jaw that he was upset not to be with the rest of them below, with the scanning equipment readouts. But he had lost all respect for Luke and Mel and Dr. Wineguard, and no matter how much pleading we had done with him to just pretend that everything was normal, he had refused.

"Magnetic information," he commented almost tonelessly. "Just like on cassette tapes."

"What would an actual magnet do to computer CDs? Back-up tapes?"

He frowned. "The CDs would be fine. They're digital. But it would erase disks or tapes completely, or at the very least distort them. The last thing you want around those things is another magnetic field."

Just like Lisa's cassette tapes had been erased. It wasn't her parents' Walkman that was broken, but the tapes. Erased.

I opened my mouth to tell him about the magnetic doorway and how Mike's bottlecap had stuck to it, when I noticed something in the mists past his shoulder.

I gulped. Not twice. Three times. And each time, my throat became drier.

"Turn slowly, pal," I finally managed to choke out.

The others caught the slow movement of my pointing arm and turned, as well.

Ahead, breaking through the mists, was the serpentine neck and head matching exactly the descriptions of the Ogopogo we'd read about.

"It can't be!" Ralphy hissed as he cocked his head to listen below. "I don't hear any beeping."

"It's on the surface," I whispered back. "The scanner must be missing it completely."

The boat glided forward. Mists swirled. Captain Luke, I'm sure, had not seen it yet.

Ralphy strained to see it better. The mist seemed to drape the figure. One moment, there. The next, not. The next, there again.

I checked back to see if Captain Luke had noticed by now.

I felt Ralphy brush against me as he strained harder to look.

Captain Luke glanced at us. I'm sure he did. It only made what happened next more chilling. Because nobody in the world will be able to convince me what happened next was an accident.

I saw the subtle movement—I know I did—of Captain Luke's arm as he jerked the engine gear into reverse. The boat lurched, and Ralphy toppled overboard into the icy mountain lake water and disappeared.

For too many heart-stopping moments, none of us reacted.

Ralphy was in water deeper than we could imagine with the suddenly real possibility of a lake monster able to pull him down forever!

Captain Luke came whipping around the side of the deck.

"I'll get him!" he shouted as he scrambled to get out of his heavy jacket. His panic, however, caused him to slip, and he banged his head against the deck, then groaned once before passing out completely.

Ralphy appeared briefly on the surface.

"G... g... get me," he sputtered weakly. "Before the monster does!"

I looked around for the rope and life preserver that had been securely in place the day before. *Nothing.* No life preservers. No rope. There was nothing in sight to throw to Ralphy.

He went under again, then fought his way to the surface.

It was not the time to wonder about missing rescue equipment.

The only plan that hit me was so terrifying I didn't dare stop to tell myself it might not work.

"Mike, grab my ankles." I said it without the fear I felt because I couldn't afford to have Mike as scared as I was.

Without waiting for his reply, I crawled to the edge of the boat.

"Lisa," I spoke quickly. "You grab, too."

With those words and the reassuring grip of hands around my ankles, I eased forward.

"Ralphy!" My voice became as urgent as I felt. A quick glance showed that the monster had not yet surged into sight again.

"Here." His voice was weaker.

I stretched my hands as far as I could, keenly aware that if Mike or Lisa's hands slipped, I, too, would be in those countless tons of deep, deep water.

Ralphy reached once and fell short. He reached again and bounced his fingers off mine. On his third try, we made contact.

I squeezed hard against his wrist, determined that not even a monster would tear him away from me.

"Okay!"

Slowly, much too slowly, they pulled both of us in.

Then stronger hands grabbed Ralphy's arms, and with a final yank, we were both aboard.

I sprawled on the deck and looked up into Captain Luke's concerned eyes.

Phony concern, I told myself. Too convenient that he fell on his way to supposedly rescuing Ralphy. Too convenient that all the rescue equipment was suddenly missing. What had Ralphy learned in the last few days that had made him one more person to get rid of?

"All okay?" Captain Luke asked.

I bit back a sharp reply and only nodded.

"Good. We'll head back right away."

"But what about the Ogopo—" Mike started to say until Lisa sharply motioned behind Luke's back with a finger across her lips. She pointed silently to the sky.

The mist was beginning to clear, and nothing marked the water except some steeply rising rocks. In the vague shape of a sea monster.

No, I told myself, *it was more than those rocks in the mist.* Whatever we saw had definitely been alive.

But now, in the clearing of the sky, I couldn't be absolutely sure.

Ralphy hiccuped. Captain Luke helped him to his feet and at the same time rubbed the back of his own head where it had banged the deck. "Come on, son," he muttered. "We'd both better see a doctor."

That's when James appeared, anger written in purple across his face.

"What's holding us up here?"

Captain Luke waved him away with a weary arm. "We're going back. Ralphy and I need to get into town."

James glared, opened his mouth to protest, then shut it again. He spun on his heel and marched back below.

When the ship docked, James marched back out again. He remained as silent as he had been earlier. Except this time he clenched a pistol in his right hand. Its sudden presence spoke loudly enough.

CHAPTER  20

Although I didn't like James much, I wanted to cheer. Whatever was about to happen next, at least our gang was safe.

His next words did not prove me wrong. "Mel, Dr. Wineguard, and Captain Luke. Don't think I'm so stupid that I don't know what you are up to. You'll do exactly as I say."

Without wavering his intense focus on the three adults, James shouted past the dock. "Lipka, it's safe to come out now."

A curtain dropped back into place, as if someone had been watching us from the motor home. Seconds later, I heard the door click open and shut, and a man appeared from around the corner.

Captain Luke groaned.

I rubbed my eyes. The man approaching us looked familiar. He was... He was... the man who had been in the bed beside James in the hospital! Yes, it *was* the man, with the distinctive ring on his massive hand still in place.

What's happening?

"The three of you, into the motor home." James motioned at Mel, Dr. Wineguard, and Captain Luke to step off the dock.

"What about the children?" Dr. Wineguard asked.

"Isn't it a little late for concern? After all, you faked the publicity thing all this time."

Faked? Had Dr. Wineguard stooped this low to use us as a cover for his own theft plans?

My answer came immediately. Dr. Wineguard looked at the ground. As if ashamed.

Ralphy tugged at my sleeve. I shook him off. It was too crucial to hear the rest.

"Yes," James continued. "Shameless of you to fool them in your attempts to fool me."

James turned to us. "Since you had nothing to do with any of this, you will not have to pay."

James spoke quietly to the man named Lipka. "Is the hard drive disconnected?"

"Ready to go."

"Good. I don't like desperate measures like this, but when Captain Luke insisted on returning, it left us with no choice."

I could imagine how desperate James felt. My guess was that Captain Luke had engineered Ralphy's fall into the water for exactly that, returning to steal the hard drive.

Lipka and Captain Luke exchanged steely stares. Lipka was the first to shrug and look away. Of course, I thought, the symbol they both shared.

"Compudel," I said as the thought came to me out of the blue. "Both of you are from Compudel." The tension among the grown-ups switched suddenly toward me, and I shrunk.

"Say that again." James narrowed his eyes.

"Um, Compudel." My thoughts were all jumbled, but James waited and the silence grew very heavy. So I tried to fill it. "Nothing was making sense about this until I realized that Lipka and Captain Luke must both belong to Compudel."

I stopped speaking. The silence continued as all of them stared at me.

I spoke quickly. "It's the ring. I suddenly realized it's a Compudel symbol. And knowing how Captain Luke and Mel and Dr. Wineguard are trying to steal the program, it makes sense."

James handed his gun to Lipka. "Take them into the motor home and tie them there. I'm going to have a discussion with the kid."

Captain Luke opened his mouth to speak, but Lipka pulled back the safety and let the click echo. Luke snapped his mouth shut and meekly followed Mel and Dr. Wineguard.

"Okay," James said as he led me to the picnic table. "Tell me everything you know. It's very important."

"Important?"

"Yes," he spat. "More important than you know. As you guessed, both of them are from the Compudel security division. How you figured what you did determines more than you can imagine."

I concentrated hard under his fierce look and told him everything. Why we suspected Mel and Dr. Wineguard and Captain Luke, right down to how I knew Ralphy going overboard wasn't an accident.

"Yes," James said grimly after spending time in silence to consider my story. "The rope and life preservers are probably in the motor home. Luke definitely had something planned. In fact, that's why Lipka has been around the entire time, looking to prove that Luke was trying to steal information while taking advantage of his position to double-cross the company."

He paused, then snapped his fingers, as if coming to a decision. "You guessed most of it right. Lipka and I finally had enough proof, and I think Luke knew it. It's a good thing Lipka was moving in this morning, or who knows what might have happened."

I nodded. "What next, sir? Straight into town and to the police?"

"Almost." James paused and thought. "The only trouble is, once they are arrested, our search for the Ogopogo is over. And from what I've been seeing with the scanner, we're very, very close to proving it's alive."

I nodded, although I was puzzled.

James said impatiently, "I want to spend the next few hours taking a final sweep of the lake. Those will be the last hours of peace. Lipka can handle taking them into town. I'll meet all of you later." He grinned. "Hopefully with proof of the monster."

Mike, Lisa, Ralphy, and Joel stood in a tight group a few yards off. Mike's twisted neck and head must have been about to fall off from trying so hard to overhear us.

James spoke again. "Can I trust you kids to wait here? I don't want you in the motor home, in case Luke tries something drastic."

"Of course, sir," I said. "I'm sorry that Dr. Wineguard had to bring us along for such terrible reasons."

"You did just fine." James squeezed my shoulder and turned abruptly to enter the motor home.

The rest of the gang crowded around me as we were left alone.

"What was all that about?" Mike asked. I explained. My throat was dry from doing so much explaining.

Ralphy finally broke in. "Ricky, I was trying to tell you something."

"Right," I said. "What?"

"You were wrong about the Scanner."

"Huh?"

Ralphy repeated, "You were wrong about the Scanner when you said the Ogopogo was too close to the surface. It should have picked up on it. That's the way it is built."

I shrugged. "It might have been one of those rocks, anyway."

"No," Ralphy said. "I don't think the program works. At all. I think it's all fake."

"So why would Dr. Wineguard go to so much effort to steal a program he knows is fake?" I asked. "Only someone who thought it was real would care about it."

James stepped outside the door, looked around briefly, and stepped back inside. *Only someone who thought it was real . . . James doesn't know the program is fake!*

"Oh no," I said.

I suddenly knew without doubt.

"Mike," I said, "when that door opens again, punch Ralphy in the stomach."

"What?!"

"No time to explain. I need a diversion—you guys fighting. It's the only thing that will work."

"Hey—" Ralphy started. Mike placed his hand on Ralphy's arm. He must have seen the seriousness and fear in my eyes. Lisa watched all of us gravely.

"I won't hit hard," Mike promised him. "Just be gentle with me in return."

I sprinted away in a low crouch, praying I would make it back with my absence undiscovered.

CHAPTER 21

I had two things to worry about. One, would Mike ever forgive me for his black eye. Two, exactly when would the motor home stop.

Only minutes earlier, I had returned to find James and Lipka—I still didn't know the big man's full name—trying to separate Ralphy and Mike.

And what a fight they had.

The only trouble was, Mike had forgotten to duck one of Ralphy's fake punches and had taken all four knuckles in the right eye socket.

His yelp of pain had been real enough for me to move unnoticed beside Lisa.

"What *is* going on?" she had hissed.

"I wish I could explain. But there's not enough time before James takes off."

So I had left her standing there less than a minute later as James moved to the boat while Lipka slipped back into the motor home to deal with his three prisoners.

What I hadn't said to Lisa was that I also wished I could be more certain I was right about being wrong before. Because my sudden realization had meant making a sprint for the bumper of the motor home as Lipka roared away, and it had meant betting my life that I had been wrong all along.

Lipka did not go easy on the gas pedal. The motor home sped up and down the hills as it moved farther and farther away from Penticton. It swayed around corners and lurched into bumps, and each time my fingerhold grew more desperate.

The whining of tires at high speed changed so abruptly that I nearly yelled. We were so far from camp now that we had hit gravel as the road narrowed.

Strangely, the humor of my situation hit me. There was only wind and exhaust and choking dust as an audience, so I had no one to share it with. Hadn't I been on the back end of this very same motor home barely a week before? Hadn't it turned out terribly because I had guessed wrong about a man with a bazooka?

Worse, I could not expect a passing police car to spot me on the bumper and rescue all of us. The road was getting higher into the hills and more remote with every mile.

I tried not to think about how much worse this situation would be if I was wrong for the final time.

Another crashing bump nearly shook me loose.

The most important question became one of hanging on for my life. I concentrated on the struggle to remain perched above the blur of gravel.

I saw my chance when Lipka crawled beneath the front end of the motor home.

The ride had taken us to the top of the hill where Lipka had slowly and painstakingly turned the motor home around so that it was facing downhill again.

Then he had parked the vehicle and slid underneath.

I carefully opened the side door, lifted one leg to enter, and—

My weight!

If I stepped into the motor home too quickly, the springs would give slightly and anyone underneath would notice!

My skin grew cold at how close I had come to being caught.

But I had to move quickly.

Instead of going feet first, I went arms first, easing myself onto the motor home floor. I held my breath.

No scurrying from below.

I closed the door behind me and only then looked up to see how excited Mel and Dr. Wineguard and Captain Luke must be to be rescued. They were bound by duct tape. I lifted my finger to my mouth to indicate they shouldn't make any noise. I moved closer, and then the springs of the motor home creaked a slight warning.

Lipka!

With only seconds to spare, I knew I could not waste a single moment.

Without stopping to worry about how badly I was trapping myself, I rolled twice and came up in front of the motor home's bathroom stall.

I hopped inside and locked the door.

CHAPTER 22

"What good do you think this is going to do?" Dr. Wineguard asked. "You guys can't unlock the master program without the access code."

"We've got it," Lipka said. "Although I have to give you credit. You didn't make it easy. For a while there, I thought we'd have to try dynamite again."

Lipka's laughter reached me clearly. "That was our first plan. Scare you enough with the discovery of the explosives that you would call off the mission. We figured once you had returned home, it would be easy enough to steal both the hardware and the software from wherever it was kept— without the suspicion falling on James. And once we had the program, James could have cracked the access code at his leisure."

Lipka paused. "But we've got the code now."

"Impossible," Wineguard said.

"Hardly. Remember the computer that James took into town? The one that he had sabotaged to make you think it needed repairs? He made an adjustment to a little gadget he'd hidden inside the computer casing. On a receiver. Look up."

I couldn't see what Lipka was pointing out, since I was hidden in the bathroom. But his voice told me all I needed to know.

"Hidden camera," Lipka said. "In a spot where it captured your keyboarding. Like a spy that let us watch you input the access code. It sends information wirelessly to the receiver hidden in the computer's case. We thought it would be a piece of cake to transmit all the information to a receiver outside the motor home, but you were clever with the scrambling devices. And that magnetic doorframe meant we couldn't just take it out on a diskette, like we'd planned. So James had to reconfigure the device to store the information on the hard drive, and then he wrote it to a compact disc."

"It was you that knocked out Ricky in the computer shop, wasn't it?"

"Cost us five hundred bucks to rent the back area and all the equipment for an afternoon of privacy," Lipka answered. "James had just finished putting some bugs in the software so that you'd have to unlock the master, and he was nearly finished putting the transmitter back into place. I couldn't afford to have the kid see him doing that and ask questions."

More laugher. Not nice laughter. "But it looks like your plan worked. You smoked out the people who were stealing information. Of course, what you didn't know is that we have a buyer in North Korea, and for what he's willing to pay for the program, we decided it's worth our while to openly steal it and disappear, especially now that we have the access code. It's going to look like a boating accident. Authorities will decide we're dead at the bottom of a bottomless lake. We're going to enjoy a very wealthy retirement in South America."

Another pause. "Oh, and you can probably guess why I'm so happy to tell you all this. Because, of course, you won't be able to pass on the information after your own little accident that I promised. You see, I have a bottle here with some stuff that will put you to sleep very quickly."

When Lipka finished telling them that, there was silence.

Then shuffling.

Just when my nerves were stretched to thin, brittle wires, the engine started. *Where are we going now?*

I heard something faint above the rumbling of the motor, something that flooded me with dread. The driver's door had opened, then closed. As if someone had stepped out. And the motor home was in motion!

I fumbled with the bathroom door and opened it a crack.

Now only Mel and Dr. Wineguard were on the cushions. Their faces were slack and blank as they slouched back in the cushions of the bench seat opposite the wall of computers.

Hey! I wanted to shout, *it's me!*

I waved frantically instead.

Nothing.

Their hands were untied and their eyes closed.

What was going on? Were they dead?

Lipka was nowhere in sight, and Captain Luke was at the wheel.

Were we free? Had Captain Luke overpowered Lipka, shoved him out the door, and taken off?

Captain Luke answered my question by slumping over the wheel. He was unconscious, too.

It doesn't take me long to figure things out. No way. Like an idiot, I stood there for another ten seconds before Lipka's plan dawned on me.

Less than two city blocks away, the road made a hairpin curve around the side of the hill. Far, far below, the lake water glittered blue.

Lipka, who had jumped out of the motorhome, was safely behind us on foot, Captain Luke was a shapeless sack at the wheel, the motor home was out of control and gathering speed, and beyond the curve were hundreds of feet of drop-off.

Maybe, just maybe, there was a reason for all of this. Like maybe they wanted the motor home to go off the cliff?

It took another half second for my body to agree with my mind.

First I yelled in sheer panic. That didn't slow the motor home at all.

I jumped forward and pulled at Captain Luke's large and heavy body.

That wasted at least one city block worth of distance.

I pushed.

That wasted a half of a city block.

And the motor home was still gaining speed and spraying gravel!

The seat! Move the seat back!

With less than ten seconds left, I found the lever on the side of the seat and shoved it back as far as I could.

I squeezed myself between Captain Luke and the steering wheel and jammed on the brakes.

The motor home began to skid sideways.

Think, Ricky, *think!* In a split second of clearness, the feel of the grass beneath these same wheels. The motor home had slewed wildly in the Jamesville park and I had . . .

I had eased off the brakes and used the steering wheel to miss the tree back then!

Gently, I took my foot away and gripped the steering wheel with strength I did not know existed.

Slowly—because each remembered second of driving in the park had reminded me of what to do—I turned the steering wheel.

The motor home groaned at the forces of gravity against gravel, but I gently applied more brakes and gritted my teeth.

The curve of the road was upon us and the motor home did not want to follow it, but the last three seconds of pumped braking slowed us enough to stay on the road.

We had made it!

From there, it was easy to stop the heavy vehicle. I pulled the gear lever into Park and squeezed back out from beneath the steering wheel.

My clothes were soaked with sweat.

Then I remembered.

Lipka!

He would have seen the motor home's brake lights flashing. He would have seen it make the corner safely.

Even as my terror subsided, he was probably running down the road!

I squeezed back in and drove—as slowly as possible—around a few more curves, then stopped again. That, I hoped, would give me enough time to move Captain Luke from behind the steering wheel.

I ran to the basin in the washroom and filled a cup of water. Three facefuls later, Captain Luke stirred slightly.

I slapped his face.

"You've got to move," I pleaded.

He finally groaned and opened his eyes.

"Ricky?!"

"Please, sir. You've got to move."

He held his head as if it were made of glass and, with more groaning, fell in the direction of the passenger seat. I pushed his legs over and left him in a pile where he landed. It was more important to get moving again.

"Go shlowly," he mumbled. "Brayshbled."

"Pardon?"

He waved his hand feebly. "Ushe low gear. Go shlow." He passed out again.

I did not understand why he wanted me to do it, but I did discover that low gear kept us from going too quickly downhill.

I discovered what he meant when we arrived at camp.

"Hey, Lisa!" I shouted proudly as we rolled up. My arm was out the window like a cool driver, and I had one hand on the steering wheel. Lisa and Mike and Ralphy jumped from their glum positions on the grass.

Joel, as usual, had more important things to do. Like move his teddy bear out of sight.

"Hey, Lisa!" I shouted again. "We're back safe!"

I waved cheerfully, and I hit the brakes one last time.

Nothing happened.

The motor home continued its slow roll.

Mike and Lisa and Ralphy dove in all directions.

The motor home drove through the picnic table, sending splinters in all directions. It drove through two bushes and still continued.

It settled knee-deep with a mild gurgle in the lake by the dock.

"Told you," Captain Luke woke up to say through heavy lips. "Brakesh were bled."

That's what Lipka was doing beneath the motor home! I realized. He had been cutting a hole in the brake lines to slowly leak all the fluid.

I thought of all the curves I had calmly driven through on the way down. And I fainted.

CHAPTER 23

I woke with my head in Lisa's cool hands and with her blue and beautifully concerned eyes searching mine.

"Heaven?" I asked. "I see an angel."

Lisa giggled.

Mike prodded me. "Get up, lazy bones."

I tried a convincing groan.

He only prodded me again. I made a mental note to speak to him sometime about jealousy. Not that I would ever admit I liked having Lisa so concerned and gentle.

We were on the grass near where the picnic table had once stood.

Mel offered me a glass with orange juice. "Luke tells me you saved our lives."

Dr. Wineguard and Captain Luke moved into my line of vision, both smiling gravely.

I began to remember. The terrifying motor-home ride and arriving safely at the bottom, only to find out the brakes could have gone any time. . . . Instead of fainting at the thought, this time I tried to be cool. "Shucks, it was nothing. But you're welcome to mention it anytime you want."

All three of them grinned back.

More of it all returned as I groggily managed to sit. "Hey!" I said. "You guys are all right!"

Mel nodded. "All it took was a little fresh air and time. We were chloroformed."

"Chloroformed?"

"Yes," Dr. Wineguard said. "It's a type of knockout liquid."

I remembered how limp and slack they had been in the motor home, how I had been afraid it was too late.

I winced as I stood. "Lipka came prepared, didn't he?"

Captain Luke nodded. "It was a smooth plan, all right. He tied us first, then knocked us out and untied us so that everything would look like an accident."

"And," Mel added, "before you snuck into the motor home, he made sure he told us every detail beforehand. Including the slow leak in the brake line. He looked at us with evil on his face and chuckled to tell us exactly how he intended to make our deaths look like an accident."

It made horrible sense.

"He couldn't leave you tied up. Anybody investigating the wreck would have noticed that right away," I guessed. "So he made sure you were helpless and put Luke behind the wheel so they would at least find a body in the driver's position."

Mel shuddered agreement. "Instead of never waking up, we found ourselves back here at camp with Mike and Ralphy and Lisa shaking us awake. Without your help . . ."

I let out a deep breath of relief to remember how close it had been. "The brake lines. Why make them leak if you were going to go over the cliff anyway?"

"Good question," Captain Luke said. "Lipka knew the wreck would be investigated. He wanted people to think we missed the corner because the brake fluid had leaked."

Mike protested. "Nobody would look that closely at the accident."

Dr. Wineguard pressed his lips tight again and shook his head in disagreement. "Sorry, Mike. You're wrong. The FBI would be going over the wreck with a fine-tooth comb."

Mike's jaw nearly hit his knees. "FBI?"

I laughed with pleasure. The last piece of the puzzle had fallen into place. "The FBI. That's you, isn't it, Mel. Captain Luke and Lipka were from Compudel's security. You're from the FBI."

Her eyes narrowed. It was enough confirmation.

"You figured that out?" Luke sputtered. His face darkened slightly, and I hoped that trace of anger was at himself, not me. In fact, a man that big was someone I didn't want knowing about the suspicions I'd first had about him.

Mike almost danced in impatience. "Ricky, you said Luke and the others were the bad guys. Now what's happening?"

Thanks, pal, I thought as I smiled weakly at Luke.

He growled a mock growl, then grinned to show he wasn't mad.

I glanced at Dr. Wineguard's raised eyebrow. "Well," I apologized in self-defense. "*Some* of my guesswork was right."

I pointed to Ralphy. "For starters, it was Ralphy who finally realized the computer program itself was a fake."

Ralphy blushed as everyone's attention turned to him.

"Come on," I said. "Explain."

"Well, we were told the scanner was built to pick up anything. There we were, among those rocks, and the blipping didn't change. As if it had been preprogrammed. As if it were a fake."

Dr. Wineguard sighed and shook his head. "I should have known better than try to get into crime fighting. I'm a scientist and that's where I should always stay."

"It was your idea, sir?" Ralphy asked. I noticed he was standing close to him again, glad, I'll bet, to have his hero back.

My little brother, Joel, remained on the beach near the half-sunken motor home, playing with an object I couldn't quite see.

"Yes, my idea, Ralphy," replied Dr. Wineguard. "I'll take total blame. You see, Compudel had been losing too many industrial secrets in research of mine. At first they suspected me."

Mel patted his shoulder. "Well, you are a bit eccentric once in a while."

Dr. Wineguard briefly lifted his other eyebrow for her benefit, then continued as if she hadn't said a word. "Some of those secrets involved underwater computer research that Compudel was doing for the military. That's when Mel was given the assignment to spy on me."

Mel laughed. "Only it didn't take long for the genius to figure out I really wasn't a marine journalist."

A chuckle from Dr. Wineguard. "So when I confronted her, we both decided it might be James. But one, we had no way of proving it, and two, without a way to prove it was him, we didn't know how he got the secrets out."

I nodded. "Because naturally, Compudel had its own security men trying to unravel things. Two men, to be exact. Captain Luke and Lipka."

"Yes. At first, I didn't know who around me to trust. Including Compudel's own security people. So I decided to pretend I had invented the most valuable underwater program of all time, something so valuable that the thief would risk almost anything to get it."

"Why the expedition, sir?" Ralphy asked. "If you knew that there was no way to actually find the Ogopogo, why go to all this trouble?"

"Two reasons. First, with a little work, I could use current graphics programs and set up a premade video that looked like actual scanning. And second, by making the Sonar Scanner so public, the thief would never suspect we were setting a trap."

He paused. "The expedition itself was legitimate. All your expenses were paid by Compudel's public relations budget. Besides, this was supposedly a nonviolent crime. We never thought you would be in danger."

That made sense. "So," I said, "when I overheard Captain Luke and Mel in the hospital talking about getting rid of James, it was actually because you were worried about our safety."

"You heard that!" Captain Luke raised a bushy blond eyebrow in surprise. "With the crazy things that had been happening, we decided it was nearly time to end the bluff and accept the fact it hadn't worked, before one of you kids was hurt. In fact, I arranged for Ralphy to fall overboard so that I'd have an excuse to send all of you home."

From the corner of my eye, I noticed Joel wander farther down the beach. He kept the object in front as he fiddled with it.

Captain Luke suddenly pointed at me. "All right. We've told you enough. Your turn. How did you figure all this out?"

First, I explained all of why I had suspected Captain Luke and Mel and Dr. Wineguard were the thieves.

As I finished, Mike suddenly banged his head with the heel of his hand.

We all stared at him.

"He's getting away," Mike said tersely. "We're standing here congratulating ourselves on how we figured everything out, and James is putting miles of water between us!"

CHAPTER 24

Captain Luke frowned. "We hadn't forgotten, Mike. Mel has already radioed the local police to watch the local marinas and roads. The most important thing is that we pinpointed the source of the leaks: James and Lipka. The second most important thing—" Captain Luke shrugged— "well, we can't have everything."

"Like their whole network?" I asked with a grin. "Who James and Lipka passed their secrets to and all that stuff?"

"Kid, you *are* spooky."

It was my turn to shrug again. "I read lots of spy novels." I did have one other secret, but I didn't want to reveal it yet. It was too much fun knowing something they didn't.

Lisa stamped her foot. "Enough. I want to know how you finally decided it was James behind all of this."

Yes, I told myself, *it is fun having her and Mel waiting for each word.*

"Well," I began slowly. "At first, when Captain Luke knocked Ralphy overboard, I thought it was proof that he was one of the bad guys."

Captain Luke put up his hands in self-defense. "I did it because I was scared James was about to try something desperate. As you know, I was looking for an excuse to get you kids back into town, so I hid all the life preservers, expecting it would be no problem to dive overboard and rescue Ralphy. Unfortunately, it only triggered James."

I shook my head. "I don't think so, sir. What triggered him was the night before. The access code."

"Access code?"

"Yes. Dr. Wineguard was concentrating so hard, he made James stand away, but he forgot to tell Mel not to watch. It tipped James off that Dr. Wineguard and Mel were a team."

"Okay," Mike announced without patience. "What else?"

I remembered what I'd heard while I was hidden in the bathroom of the motor home. "The magnetic doorway was set up to erase any data that a thief might try to take out on a magnetic disk or tape."

Wineguard nodded. "Even though much of the program was fake, there was enough in it that was too valuable to risk getting stolen."

"And the cell phones," I said. "They don't work in the motor home, either. Was that because of the scrambler that Lipka mentioned?"

Wineguard nodded again. "We have a scrambler set up. Blocks any possibility of a wireless transfer from the inside going out. Or wireless hacking from the outside going in."

"I can't figure out the poison," I said. "If James did this to get all of us out of the way, why would he eat a bowl that he knew was poisoned?"

It was Mel's turn to speak. "I can. He cut himself chopping the onions. Probably took a bowl for himself out of the pot before adding the poison. That way when we saw him eating it, we'd say exactly what you just did. Why eat from chili that you've poisoned yourself?"

I remembered what Dr. Wineguard had told me in the hospital. The poison couldn't be absorbed through the skin, and it was only dangerous if I'd had any cuts on my legs.

"He accidentally poisoned himself through the cut," I said. "Right?"

"Yes," Mel said. "I don't feel sorry for him."

We found out later that when Lipka had found out James was in the hospital, he'd arranged to get a bed beside him so that they could plan their next steps. As for Captain Luke, he thought he could oversee everything from his "hidden" position as boat captain. He also thought his partner, Lipka, would watch everything else from the outside. What Captain Luke of course did not know was that Lipka was also in partnership with James.

Dr. Wineguard knew at that point that this was what James was trying to do, but he still had no proof. Which was why he hadn't called the police when he first discovered the dynamite. He wanted to keep the expedition going forward so that their own security people could catch James. It made me shiver, realizing that the entire game had been played coldly and silently while our gang was supposed to think it was just a fun summer trip.

But Dr. Wineguard was worried about us despite the game being so well hidden. That's why he warned me away from the shop. I managed to get in the way anyhow, just as Lipka was about to leave, but unfortunately I decided Mel or Luke had knocked me out.

When I finished explaining everything in the sunshine of that morning, Mike still was not satisfied.

"You still risked too much. What if you were wrong? How could you get on the bumper of that motor home after being so stupid about it the week before?"

I held up two fingers. "One, Dr. Wineguard himself had told me 'Better safe than sorry' when I first put his motor home in the pond."

"And the second?" Lisa asked.

"My head," I said. "Feel these stitches."

She frowned and did so. "A small circle."

I nodded. "From a big ring. When Lipka punched me to knock me out in the computer shop, his ring cut my skin. That was the last clue I needed. Remembering his ring."

And that was it.

Except for the surprise I had saved for last.

"By the way," I said as casually as possible, "remember the fight I asked Ralphy and Mike to start?"

"How could I forget?" Mike said sourly. "My eye is still sore."

Ralphy grinned. It was not too often he managed to get Mike a good one.

"Well," I announced triumphantly, "I skipped back to the boat."

Suddenly Captain Luke leaned forward. "Yes?"

"I cut one of the hydraulic cables from the boat's steering wheel, one of the ones you showed me earlier."

Captain Luke started laughing. "Get out of here. You mean . . . you mean . . ."

I nodded. Dr. Wineguard and Mel looked strangely at us.

"I mean," I said, "that the boat is in the middle of the lake, going in circles. With James stuck on it."

I puffed out my chest and gave a pose that any hero would be proud of.

Then I noticed what Joel was playing with.

"Aaaawk!" I started running. "Get my camera away from the water!"

I tripped over the broken picnic table and hit my head on the ground. When they picked me up, they had to take me back to the hospital for complete restitching.

Epilogue

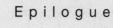

All I can tell anyone in Jamesville is that no speedboats were near our camp that day.

Mike, who stayed behind as they took me to the hospital, is willing to bet his entire baseball card collection on it.

He would have noticed, too. After all, he was hoping for the boat to appear so that he could be the first one to spot James and his endless circling.

But no boat.

They did find James, though. The boat had run out of gas, and he sat there to be plucked from the lake like a tied duck.

James made the mistake of not recognizing his rescuers as policemen until too late. They caught him throwing a small notebook overboard, and it floated long enough to be netted. Even after the ink had run, there was enough information for the authorities to track down the North Korean source that had been willing to buy the program.

As for us, Compudel decided that no publicity about two in-company spies was the best type of publicity.

So all the public ever found out was that the Ogopogo hunt was an expensive failure.

In Jamesville, we took quite a bit of ribbing about it. And, bound by secrecy, we could tell no one what really happened.

That was almost the worst part.

Because I will always believe the expedition was a success.

First, it was a success because Dr. Wineguard answered my question about science and how it fit with believing in God.

There, overlooking the lake and standing by ourselves, he had surprised me by asking me a question. "Ricky," he had smiled, "why is it important you know?"

I had shifted from foot to foot. "Sometimes it seems that nothing in our science textbooks mentions God. If He's behind everything, shouldn't that be obvious even in science?"

"Ah," he said thoughtfully, then had gazed at the hills that lined the lake. "You might not know this, but every time scientists find a new answer, a dozen more questions occur. For example, you've heard of atoms and molecules, the tiny, tiny particles that make up all substances?"

I nodded.

"Well, scientists know that electricity holds them together, but they don't know *why*.

"Here's another example. Doctors can detail every step of the growth of a baby, from the moment it is conceived to the day it is born. But modern medicine still cannot explain the miracle of *why*, at the moment of conception, a new life is created."

I dimly began to understand. "We're back to 'how' versus 'why.'"

"Yup," Dr. Wineguard said. "Science explores 'how.' Many of the greatest scientists in the world are men and women of great faith. The more they dig into the mysteries of science, the more they discover and understand that God truly is behind everything. They've studied for years, and they see that behind 'how' everything works, there is the handiwork of God's design and power. These scientists know more than anyone that science and God are not separate."

Dr. Wineguard caught my slight nod of understanding.

"Yes," he continued, "It's just unfortunate that many of your science textbooks only address half the question, which, of course, is the 'how' of science. The more advanced books will tell you that the closer scientists get to answering all the 'hows,' the more perplexed they become at the 'why,' which as we know comes from God."

Then there had been a friendly silence between us, broken only by the sound of leaves rustling in a slight breeze.

"I'm nearly finished," he smiled, "but I'm glad you asked your question. I want to answer it as thoroughly as possible.

"Remember this: The Bible is not a scientific manual. It is a book as old as civilization, written about God and His relationship with humans. Since the Bible is not a scientific manual—but rather an awesome book with stirring and divine poetry and literature—you *cannot* ask of it scientific questions. To do so makes as little sense as approaching your science book with difficult philosophical 'why' questions."

I understood! It disappeared, that vague unease within me that either the Bible was right or scientists were right. I *could* accept many things in science and know that God was behind everything.

Then he had bowed and said with a flourish, "Now, if my little lecture is finished, we should hurry to join the rest of the gang. I have a feeling that we've left Joel alone too long already."

Which made me grin more. Even Dr. Wineguard knew that leaving Joel alone for five minutes was five minutes too many.

Which also gives one other reason the expedition had been a success. The photograph.

You see, because all the stitches had broken loose from my fall, and because blood was going in all directions, everybody forgot about Joel and the camera.

By the time I returned from the hospital to snatch it from him— six months of paper delivery for an automatic-focus camera and he was juggling it like an orange—he had managed to waste an entire roll of snapshots.

Mike, supposedly guarding Joel, hadn't cared. Instead, he was at the end of the dock with binoculars, peering in the distance to watch for James.

In a way, then, the joke was on Mike. The poor guy missed

something right under his nose that Joel didn't.

At least, that's what we think.

Because the second-to-the-last photograph of thirty-six shows something that still takes my breath away.

It frames a deep wake in the water. That's all. A deep wake and what, if you look close enough, may be the end of something round and thick and rubbery looking.

I say it's the Ogopogo.

So does Mike. He *knows* no boats went by to leave a wake in the water like that. In fact, Mike nearly cries with frustration to think about how close he was to seeing it.

Not many people in Jamesville think much of the photo, though, because it was taken by a six-year-old and doesn't show enough to really make for proof.

Only Joel knows for sure. And he, of course, isn't telling.

Around the World With Christian Heroes!

TRAILBLAZER BOOKS give you an adventure story, an introduction to a Christian hero of the past, and a look at a time and place that will fascinate you. Whatever country or time interests you most, chances are there's a TRAILBLAZER BOOK about it. And, each story is told through the eyes of a boy or girl your age. Be sure to travel the globe and go back through time with the TRAILBLAZER BOOKS.

TRAILBLAZER BOOKS by Dave and Neta Jackson

Abandoned on/Wild Frontier - Cartwright
Ambushed in Jaguar Swamp - Grubb
Assassins in the Cathedral - Kivengere
Attack in the Rye Grass - Whitman
The Bandit of Ashley Downs - Müller
The Betrayer's Fortune - Simons
Blinded by the Shining Path - Sauñe
Caught in the Rebel Camp - Douglass
The Chimney Sweep's Ransom - Wesley
Danger on the Flying Trapeze - Moody
Defeat of the Ghost Riders - Bethune
Drawn by a China Moon - Moon
The Drummer Boy's Battle - Nightingale
Escape From the Slave Traders - Livingstone
Exiled to the Red River - Garry
The Fate of the Yellow Woodbee - Saint
Flight of the Fugitives - Aylward
The Forty-Acre Swindle - Carver
The Gold Miner's Rescue - Jackson
The Hidden Jewel - Carmichael

Hostage on the Nighthawk - Penn
Imprisoned in the Golden City - Judson
Journey to the End of the Earth - Seymore
Kidnapped by River Rats - Booth
Listen for the Whippoorwill - Tubman
Mask of the Wolf Boy - Goforth
The Mayflower Secret - Bradford
The Queen's Smuggler - Tyndale
Quest for the Lost Prince - Morris
Race for the Record - Ridderhof
Risking the Forbidden Game - Cary
Roundup of the Street Rovers - Brace
The Runaway's Revenge - Newton
Shanghaied to China - Taylor
Sinking the Dayspring - Paton
Spy for the Night Riders - Luther
The Thieves of Tyburn Square - Fry
Traitor in the Tower -Bunyan
Trial by Poison - Slessor
The Warrior's Challenge - Zeisberger

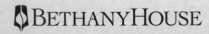

BETHANYHOUSE

11400 Hampshire Ave S. Minneapolis, MN 55438
www.bethanyhouse.com